Holding Holly

Also by Julie Brannagh

Catching Cameron
Rushing Amy
Blitzing Emily

Holding Holly

A LOVE AND FOOTBALL NOVELLA

JULIE BRANNAGH

AVONIMPULSE
An Imprint of HarperCollinsPublishers

Excerpt from *Blitzing Emily* © 2014 by Julie Revell Benjamin.
Excerpt from *Rushing Amy* © 2014 by Julie Revell Benjamin.
Excerpt from *Catching Cameron* © 2014 by Julie Revell Benjamin.
Excerpt from *Covering Kendall* © 2014 by Julie Revell Benjamin.
Excerpt from *An Heiress for All Seasons* copyright © 2014 by Sharie Kohler.
Excerpt from *Intrusion* copyright © 2014 by Charlotte Stein.
Excerpt from *Can't Wait* copyright © 2013 by Jennifer Hopkins. This novella originally appeared in the anthology *All I Want for Christmas Is a Cowboy*.
Excerpt from *The Laws of Seduction* copyright © 2014 by Gwen T. Weerheim-Jones.
Excerpt from *Sinful Rewards 1* copyright © 2014 by Cynthia Sax.
Excerpt from *Sweet Cowboy Christmas* copyright © 2014 by Candis Terry.

EPub Edition DECEMBER 2014 ISBN: 9780062363862

Print Edition ISBN: 9780062363879

AM 10 9 8 7 6 5 4 3 2

To Judi, because Santa Claus
doesn't always wear a bright red suit and
sport a long white beard.

Acknowledgments

I WANT TO thank my wonderful editor, Amanda Bergeron, for all of her hard work and her enthusiasm. It's book #5, and I am still pinching myself that she chose my books. I'd also like to thank my terrific agent, Sarah Younger of Nancy Yost Literary Agency, who chose my books too. Sarah works hard on my behalf. We bonded over our shared love of football, and I am so lucky to have her.

I'd like to thank the Avon Books art department for a cover I fell in love with, among other things. I'd also like to thank the copyediting group, especially Beverly, who keeps all of my grammar and punctuation issues on the down-low.

I'd like to thank my husband, Eric, for a million reasons, but most of all because he made sure I could pursue the thing I wanted most in life. I love you, honey.

Amy Raby and Jessi Gage (the Cupcake Crew!) are my critique partners, my Friday standing dates, and my biggest cheerleaders. I wuv you both too.

Thank you to Greater Seattle RWA. Thank you so much for your friendship, your encouragement, and for all the chocolate. I owe all of you more than I could ever say.

I'd like to thank Tiffany's. I hope to be able to afford to shop there in the near future.

As always, thank you to former and current Seattle Seahawks for interviews they've given in various forms of media that were a huge help in my research. I named my hero after one of the most inspiring players in the NFL, Derrick Coleman. I hope he won't mind.

Would you like to "adopt" a local letter to Santa Claus and brighten a child's holiday? It's as easy as appearing at your local post office and presenting a photo ID. The procedure is outlined here: https://about.usps.com/corporate-social-responsibility/letters-to-santa.htm#p=1.

Here's to the happiest of holidays for all my readers, and a wonderful and prosperous New Year for you and all those you love.

Go Sharks!

Chapter One

DERRICK COLLINS HAD two jobs today: to smile, and to sign the credit card receipts.

Derrick's mama and grandma had been asking—well, nagging—him to join them for a trip to Noel, Washington, for the past couple of years. If they went on his Tuesday off from the Sharks, they might have fun, and he might not have to sign a hundred autographs before they left the parking lot. Hopefully he'd have the element of surprise; nobody expected a six-foot-five, three-hundred-pound male in a place he imagined was dominated by females 365 days a year.

The first week of December was prime time to spend a few hours in a snow-dusted holiday paradise. Noel was a little town a hundred miles east of Seattle that had arisen from the ruins of a former logging town. The city fathers believed that "all Christmas, all the time" might be a way to bring tourism and the resulting jobs to the area. Surprisingly enough, their idea paid off in a big way.

People came from around the world to visit Noel's charming little shops, restaurants, and the town square, which boasted live holiday music year-round. The post office hand-cancelled hundreds of thousands of holiday cards with their distinctive postmark each year. The town's location also helped with the wintry weather theme: Noel featured ice and snow from October until April each year. When it wasn't snowing, there was a countdown-to-Christmas clock in the square, and Santa made an appearance on a raft in the river during the Christmas in July festival. It was fun for kids of all ages, including a defensive tackle for the Sharks and the two women who had made sure that he'd gotten his ass through college and who still kept him out of trouble.

Derrick's mama and grandma were currently in the quilt shop, which appeared to be every crafter's fantasy. He didn't understand why they took a perfectly nice piece of fabric, cut it up, and sewed it together again, but they'd gotten involved in a program which provided "baby" quilts to low-income new mothers through one of the local hospitals. Mama and Grandma's sewing machines were going day and night as a result, whenever they weren't at church or watching his grandma's beloved mixed martial arts broadcasts. He couldn't figure out why a woman who identified as a pacifist couldn't wait to watch some guy beat the crap out of another guy.

He strolled through the front door of the quilt shop and up to the counter. The woman behind the cash register looked a little scared, he thought. He towered over her. Maybe she was startled by his sheer bulk and his long dreadlocks.

"Hi. I'm Derrick Collins." He nodded toward his mama and grandma. "They're with me. Please make sure they buy whatever they want. Here's my card for their tab."

He handed her his platinum American Express card. She took it with shaking fingers. He noticed she was wearing a wedding set on the third finger of her left hand. Maybe he should encourage the cashier to call her husband and ask him if he knew who Derrick Collins was; a couple thousand bucks was walking-around money for him.

"May I...may I please see your ID?" she asked. She must not have been a football fan, Derrick thought.

"Sure," he said. He held out his driver's license to her.

She looked at the photo, glanced at the card once more, flipped it over to look at his signature, and said, "Thank you very much."

"Thank you. And I meant it: whatever my mama and grandma want."

She nodded. At the rate the women cutting fabric and gathering notions a few feet away were going, they were already up to four figures.

"Is there a place close by I could get something to drink?" he asked.

"There's a coffee shop across the hall that also sells wine and beer," she said.

"Mama," he called out. "I'll be across the hall if you need me."

"Okay, honey. We won't be long," she said.

Sure, they wouldn't. He grinned to himself. They were going to shop until they dropped, and they'd fall asleep in the back of his Escalade as he drove them home. He'd get a pizza and play some video games with a few of his teammates tonight. Mama and Grandma would eat a light dinner at his place and spend some time excitedly planning their next projects.

He pretended like they drove him nuts, but nothing could be further from the truth. He should buy them a little house somewhere peaceful in the Seattle area where they could have some privacy when they were in town, but he had to admit that he enjoyed their fussing over him. They spent most of football season in Seattle, staying in his downtown Bellevue condo. The rest of their year they spent in his tiny hometown in Alabama. They'd started visiting him a lot more often after his last relationship came to a disastrous end.

He'd dated Jada for three years. It wasn't working, but he didn't want to be alone. She started hinting around about a ring, and he finally summoned the guts to break it off. He should never have asked her for a second date. She didn't like his mama or his grandma, and the feeling was mutual. She thought his money was hers to spend. She was more interested in the fact that she was welcomed into the most exclusive nightclubs with him than she was in actually being with him.

She was the latest in a long line of women who had no interest in who he was. All they wanted was what he— and his money—could do for them. He realized he was not alone with this problem; it happened to most professional athletes. He seemed to be having trouble figuring out how to fix it, however.

"Your picker's broken, honey," his grandma had said to him more than once. "You need a nice girl. You're not going to meet your future wife and the mama of your children in a nightclub."

"But, Grandma, it's hard to meet women." The second the words left his lips, he realized he'd really stepped in it. It wasn't hard to meet women. It was hard to meet the *right* woman.

"Come to church with us. There's plenty of nice girls there," his mama said. "My friend Mavis's granddaughter is such a sweet girl. She's about to graduate from the University of Washington, and she already owns a business. If you don't like her, there are several more young women you might enjoy spending time with there."

"Oh, yes, Derrick. We'll also ask the pastor to pray that you'll find the right young lady," his grandma said. He was cooked now. The information would hit the church's prayer chain, someone would call or e-mail one of the local media, and he'd be the laughing stock of the Sharks' locker room.

"Grandma, you don't have to do that—"

"We want you to find the perfect young lady to join our family," his grandma said. "We can't wait to meet her."

He couldn't wait to meet her, either. If she existed at all.

HOLLY REYNOLDS PLUNKED herself down on a bar stool behind the counter of Caffeine Addiction, Noel's coffee shop. Baristas started their day before the sun came up, and her shift didn't end for another two hours. The business was typically crowded with tourists and locals. The owners had introduced wine, beer, and small bites last year, which drove profits even higher. Today, things were surprisingly quiet. Even the people who hid out in the back of the shop to work on their laptops had something else to do this afternoon. She was caught up on the cleaning and the million-and-one things to do while working in a coffee shop, so she had a few minutes to herself as a result.

Holly was in her last year of nursing school and on holiday break from the UW. She worked at least two jobs year-round to pay her tuition. She was trying to get out of school with the minimum to repay in student loans; she was also living with her grandma in Noel for the next couple of months. The owner of Caffeine Addiction was happy to hire an experienced barista for Noel's ultra-busy holiday season. Holly wasn't thrilled about wearing an elf costume to work every morning, but money was money.

She reached into the backpack she stowed under the counter and pulled a small stack of letters out of it. Maybe she could read a few of them while the shop was slow and make a few notes about what she'd like to say to each letter writer in response. She opened the first letter with care, pulling out a folded sheet of notebook paper with crayoned drawings of Santa Claus, an animal the child probably thought looked like a reindeer but actually resembled a moose, and Santa's sleigh.

Every November 1, the Noel Merchants' Association erected a mailbox in the town square so local children could drop their letters to Santa Claus inside. Holly's grandmother had been secretly answering those letters by hand for thirty years now. When the merchants' association urged her grandma to join the twenty-first century and establish a website to answer the letters by e-mail, Holly's grandmother refused.

"Kids wait for mail," she'd said. "I can't disappoint them."

Unfortunately, Grandma was recovering from carpal tunnel surgery this year. She was unable to handwrite the letters, so she'd asked Holly to help her with Noel's beloved holiday tradition.

Handwriting a hundred or so letters was an additional time commitment Holly didn't have, but she'd make it work. She'd stuck some of the letters in her backpack earlier, hoping maybe she could read a few of them while the shop was slow and make a few notes about what to say to each letter writer in response.

The letter featuring the crayon drawings was sweet. A little girl wanted a new bike from Santa and assured him that she'd been "very good." That would be an easy one to write. The next letter was from a little boy who wanted a baseball mitt, a new bat, and some cleats. He promised to make sure he left some carrots for the reindeer, as well as cookies for Santa: another fun letter to write.

Holly grinned to herself. This would be more fun than work. She slid her finger under the flap of the third letter and drew out a piece of unadorned notebook paper.

This one wasn't quite so cute and funny.

Dear Santa Claus,

I realize I'm too old to still believe in you, but I really need your help.

My mom told my little brother and sister that you might not be coming to our house this year. Our dad left us, and my mom lost her job. Would you please bring my brother and sister some presents? They don't know our mom doesn't have a lot of money right now. Also, I know it's a lot to ask, but would you please bring my mom a job?

Thank you so much. I hope you have a Merry Christmas.

Michael

Holly reread the letter, and her vision blurred with tears. She grabbed up the envelope. No return address. No last name. She wondered what she could do to help Michael and his family. But first, she'd have to find them. Noel wasn't a large town, but someone in this kind of trouble wouldn't be advertising it to their neighbors and friends.

Her grandma had always told her that the letters were cheerful. Noel didn't have underprivileged children—or so most people thought. Not everyone who worked in Noel was wealthy. Maybe Michael's family fell through the cracks of a town that was unrelentingly cheerful and upbeat. People came to Noel to forget their problems, not to encounter more of them.

She brushed tears off of her face with impatient fingertips and looked at the letter one more time. Michael had left no other identifying information.

"Where can I find you, Michael?" she murmured.

A few seconds later a shadow fell across the counter in front of her, and she looked up into a familiar face. Her heart skipped a beat. One of her many jobs was serving in the cafeteria at the Seattle Sharks' training camp each summer, and Derrick Collins, the guy she'd had a highly secret and raging crush on for the past two years, was standing less than a foot away from her.

If she didn't already know he was as shy as she was, she would have been scared of him. He was over a foot taller than she was, and he outweighed her by at least a hundred pounds. He wore dreadlocks, multicarat diamond stud earrings, and the latest designer denim. He got paid to manhandle other big guys six months a year. When he came through the food line at the Sharks' training facility, however, he spoke to her in a soft tone of voice and she'd seen him blush more than once.

She was wearing an elf costume. Her eyes were probably red. She felt her face getting hot. He probably thought she was a dork, and she glanced down in embarrassment.

"You look like my Holly from the food line," he said. "I haven't seen you for a while."

"Yes, it's me," she said and swallowed hard. *His* Holly. Maybe she was hearing things.

"What's the matter, Holly? How can I help?"

His bleached white smile was dazzling against his smooth ebony skin. He reached out to tip her chin up with gentle fingers.

"I'm okay." She grabbed the letters and shoved them back into her backpack. "I'm surprised to see you," she said.

"It's nice to see you too. I usually have to get up pretty early to see your smiling face." He sat down on one of the barstools on the other side of the counter. "I didn't know you lived in Noel." She saw color rising in his cheeks. "I'd come here more often."

He couldn't *really* be flirting with her. Maybe he was just trying to get her to not cry in front of him anymore or something.

"My grandma lives here. She had surgery and she needed some help, so here I am."

"That's pretty nice of you," he said. "How is she doing?"

"She'll be fine in a few weeks." She gave him a nod. He was still grinning at her.

"Will you be here until school starts again?"

"Yes," she said. She wanted to ask him what he was doing in Noel, but maybe she should try to remember she was at work first. "Would you like some coffee or a snack? We have these really great cinnamon rolls..."

He stood and moved to the barstool directly across from her. "If you have a to-go container, I'll take three. I heard y'all have beer."

"We do. We have bottles, or two local microbrews on tap." She slid off of her barstool and got him a glass of ice water. "There's Noel IPA or Black Bear Stout. Which would you like?"

"I'll take the IPA, please." He took a sip of the ice water she'd put in front of him. "You're probably wondering why I'm here."

"You could be shopping for gifts or getting your holiday cards hand-cancelled," she teased.

"I hate shopping. My mama and my grandma love it, though. They're currently buying out the quilt shop." He shook his head a little. "I told them to leave some stuff for everyone else in the candy shop earlier."

"That candy shop's a tough one to walk away from," Holly said. "They must be stocking up for the holidays." She poured his beer and put it down on a bar napkin in front of him.

"They bought some candy for me, too," he said, and she watched a faint wash of pink move over his cheeks again. "I might have a sweet tooth."

This was officially the longest conversation she'd ever had with Derrick. It was hard to imagine how such a big, tough man could exude boyish charm. He took a sip of his beer and glanced around the coffee shop. "I must have scared everyone else off."

"That's not true." She knew she should be cleaning something or straightening up. "It's been slow today." She grabbed one of the laminated menus out of the holder at the end of the counter. "Would you like something to eat?"

He took the menu out of her hand and glanced at it for a few seconds. He laid it back down on the counter and looked into her eyes. "I'd rather have something to eat with you."

The breath caught in her throat. He couldn't really mean it. Maybe he was just being nice. "I have to work right now…"

"Do you work tomorrow, too?"

"I'll be here for breakfast and lunch."

"Let's have dinner together, then." He gave her a confident grin. "Somewhere else."

Chapter Two

DERRICK WATCHED HOLLY's mouth curve into a shy smile. He'd had a thing for her since the first time he saw her dishing up breakfast to the cafeteria line at the Sharks' training camp, and he wasn't letting this chance to get to know her better slip by. She glanced into his face and back down at the counter as she thought of an answer. He wasn't going to wait.

"Do you like Mexican food?" he asked.

She nodded and forced out something that sounded like "Yes." The happiness on her face and the blush spreading over her pale skin told him she was interested, but shy. He reached out to squeeze her hand and marveled at how small it was inside of his.

"Great. I'll pick you up at six tomorrow night, then."

"But…but you don't have an address…"

He dug in his pocket for his smartphone. "If you type your address in here, I'll find your place."

She swallowed hard, blushed a little more, and wouldn't meet his eyes. "You'll be meeting my grandma. I'm at her house."

"Maybe she'd like to come to dinner, too," he teased. "I'll bring my mama and my grandma. She'll feel right at home."

She looked up into his eyes, and his heart did a funny little ba-bump as laughter spilled out of her. He wondered what he could say to her to make her laugh again.

"It sounds like quite a date," she said.

"So, that means I have one?"

"Yes." Her eyes sparkled. "I promise I won't wear the elf outfit."

His eyes held hers. "I wouldn't mind," he teased.

Derrick managed to hustle his mama and grandma out of the quilt shop before he had to call his banker and tell him to brace for incoming. They walked along Main Street, window-shopping and enjoying the chilly afternoon. It was snowing again. He loved the delight in his grandma's face as she caught a few flakes in her out-stretched hand. Snow was a rarity in Alabama.

His mama indicated the Caffeine Addiction bakery box in his hand. "Did you get some coffee beans, honey?"

"I got us some cinnamon rolls for tomorrow morning. I thought you might like them."

His grandma slipped her hand through his arm. "That sounds delicious. Are you hungry?"

"If you and Mama would like to get a bite, I'm sure I could eat."

The two women in his life tugged him through the doorway of the local diner.

"Maybe we could visit the Christmas decorations store after lunch," his mama said. He resisted the impulse to groan aloud.

DERRICK WAS SPARED from the holiday decorations store when the diner's server—a lifelong Sharks fan, she told him—asked for an autograph. Minutes later, he and his family were surrounded by clamoring football fans. Despite the best efforts of the diner's manager to persuade the other customers to let Derrick and his family eat in peace, it wasn't going to happen. Derrick glanced out the front window of the diner to note more fans gathering outside on the sidewalk too. Holly wouldn't have told people they were in town, so someone else had, and now he needed to make a quick exit.

Talking with Sharks fans was part of his job description. Normally, he loved it. He didn't enjoy seeing his mama and grandma jostled by overeager fans, or missing their chance to order a late lunch, however. He signed autographs and posed for photos while the diner's manager brought his mama and grandma something to drink and made sure they were safely away from the crowd while they waited for him.

A quick glance outside showed the line of fans stretching down the sidewalk. A woman his mom's age extended a scrap of paper to him for an autograph.

"It's so nice to see you here. My family loves the Sharks."

"We love your family, too," he said. Her face lit up.

She glanced down for a moment and bashfully peered up at him beneath her lashes.

"You probably don't want to do this in public, but I would love to see your sack dance again."

Derrick's sack dance was the toast of sports broadcasters everywhere. He'd initially done it after being egged on by one of his teammates. His belly rolls after dragging some other team's quarterback to the turf had gotten more elaborate over the years. He'd even incorporated something called a "samba roll" after briefly dating a ballroom dancing instructor. Other guys did stuff like flex their biceps, drop to one knee and pantomime roping a calf, or nothing at all. Derrick's gyrations brought wild applause and laughter around the league. And five million hits on YouTube.

"I always do this in front of thousands," he assured the woman. He called out, "Who's going to join me?"

Amid clapping and shouts of "Go Sharks!" he gave his best example. A few people jumped out of their seats to dance with him. He had to laugh when he saw his mama trying to do a belly roll too. He signed a few more autographs and posed for some more photos, then glanced around as he heard a loud voice say, "Okay, folks, let's break it up here. Mr. Collins and his family might want to have something to eat."

Noel's twelve-man police force had arrived on the scene. Within a few minutes, four uniformed officers ensured the other customers were back at their tables. Eight other officers were dispersing the crowd outside of the restaurant. One of the officers told him, "We have a squad car outside to take you back to your car, if you'd like."

"I would appreciate that. Thank you for offering," he said.

The manager of the diner walked out of the kitchen with two to-go bags. "This is for you and your family," he told Derrick. "We're sorry for the inconvenience, and we hope you'll enjoy it."

Derrick could only imagine the headlines on sports websites around the country about accepting food he didn't pay for at a local mom-and-pop-type restaurant. He grabbed his wallet out of his back pocket and pulled out three twenties. "Will this take care of it?"

"Don't worry about it. It's on the house. We hope you'll come by another time," the manager said.

"I insist," Derrick said. "We'll visit again soon." He pushed the cash into the guy's hand. "Thanks for the food."

A couple of the officers were helping his mama and grandma out of their seats. They were ushered out the front door of the diner and into the squad car seconds later amid more applause and chants of "Go Sharks!" from the crowds on the other side of the sidewalk. A few minutes later, they were in his SUV and driving toward the freeway.

"I'm sorry we didn't go to the decorations store. Maybe we could go another time," he said.

"I'm never going to get used to that," his grandma mused. "All you did was walk into the restaurant, and everyone went crazy."

"Grandma, it's football season. The team's winning, so everybody wants to talk to us." He pulled in a deep breath. "I feel bad you didn't get to see everything you wanted to see."

His grandma stifled a yawn behind one hand. "We saw plenty, honey. Thank you for taking us. We had fun, didn't we?"

"Oh, yes," his mother said. "We have so many projects now. We can visit Noel another time."

He knew they weren't trying to make him feel guilty, but he felt the pang anyway. They didn't ask for a hundred people interrupting their day out with him today.

Twenty minutes or so later, they were both fast asleep in the back seat of his SUV. He wanted to tell them about his date with Holly, but it would have to wait. He was also sure it would end up on the church's prayer chain.

LATER THAT DAY, the temperature was dropping in Noel. The town was expected to get three inches of new snow overnight. Three inches of snow would paralyze hilly Seattle, but those who lived in Noel spent all winter dealing with it. More snow meant more tourism, and more money in the pockets of local merchants.

Holly unlocked the front door of the house and called out, "Grandma, I'm home," as she stepped inside. Her grandma kept the house a toasty seventy-two degrees. Holly pulled off her down jacket and scarf as quickly as possible. She also unlaced her snow boots and stepped out of them. Her grandma didn't like anyone to wear shoes in the house.

"I'm in here," Grandma said. "How was your day?"

"It was slow until twenty minutes before I was supposed to leave." Holly kissed Grandma's cheek and sat down in the shabby, overstuffed chair next to the worn couch her grandma was sitting on. "That's why I'm late."

"The tourists are back?"

"I don't think they ever left, Grandma." She'd managed to put one very special tourist out of her mind while she finished her shift, but he was back with a vengeance the minute she got in her car to drive away. She still couldn't believe she finally had a date with Derrick Collins. She'd wanted him to ask for months.

Her grandma let out a laugh. "Did you get something to eat already?"

"I had oatmeal this morning."

"That's not enough," Grandma scolded. "Would you like me to make you a sandwich?"

"You can't use your hand yet. I'll do it. Would you like me to fix something for you, too? How about a toasted cheese sandwich?" Her grandma waved one hand in the air in a *no, thank you* gesture. "How are you feeling today?"

"Bored," Grandma said.

Her surgeon was taking the most conservative route: rest for two weeks post-surgery, and at least two months in which Grandma couldn't engage in her favorite activity, knitting. Grandma's employees were running her store, Yarn with Heart, while she spent time recuperating. She'd been home for three days, and she was already climbing the walls. Well, she'd be climbing the walls if she could use her hands to do it.

Holly sat forward in her chair a bit. "A couple of interesting things happened today."

Grandma grinned at her. "Is that so? Tell me about it."

"I have a date."

"That's wonderful, sweetie. Who are you going out with?"

Holly wanted to jump out of the chair with excitement. She fidgeted a bit.

"I met this guy named Derrick at the Sharks' training camp. He's kind of shy and sweet. I've liked him for a long time, but I didn't think he really noticed me. He was at the quilt shop earlier with his mom and grandma, and he came in to get a beer while they were shopping." She looked into her grandma's amused face. "We were alone in the coffee shop for almost an hour, and he asked me out for dinner tomorrow night."

"Derrick. Do I know him?" Grandma asked. She watched football; she could identify the team's quarterback and maybe a couple of other guys, but she probably didn't know who Derrick was at all.

"He's the big guy with the dreadlocks who does the belly roll dances every time he tackles the other team's quarterback."

"Of course I know who he is," Grandma said. "*He's* 'sweet and shy'?"

"Wait until you meet him. You'll see," Holly said. She was so excited about the date, but she let out a breath. Grandma wasn't going to be happy about the rest of her news.

"There's one more thing. He caught me crying over one of the Santa letters."

"What? How did this happen?" Grandma said. "Why were you upset?"

Holly got up from the chair, found her backpack, extracted Michael's letter, and brought it back to her grandma to read.

"The first couple of letters were so sweet, and this one is heartbreaking. I don't know what to say to him."

Holly sat down in the chair again and waited for her grandma to finish reading. When Grandma glanced up, there were tears in her eyes too.

"Do you still have the envelope the letter came in?"

"There's no address, Grandma. There's nothing written on the outside of the envelope except 'Santa Claus, North Pole.'" Holly let out a sigh. "How will we find him?"

Grandma glanced back down at the letter. "We'll find him, honey. Don't worry about that."

Chapter Three

THE NEXT DAY, Holly rifled through her closet one more time. Unfortunately, the perfect casual-but-dressy outfit for her date with Derrick didn't jump out at her. The ice and snow outside weren't compatible with the little black dress she'd brought to her grandma's for the hell of it. Noel's Mexican restaurant also wasn't a place anyone typically wore a dress to.

The women Derrick usually dated probably had a closetful of designer clothes and some really expensive shoes to wear with them. She wanted to dazzle him, but she didn't have the wardrobe to pull it off. She was still dressing in thrift shop chic and other people's hand-me-downs, and would be until she got the last of her college loans paid off.

The worn jeans and sweater that Holly pulled out of her closet would almost look presentable for a date if she put on some makeup and did a little something extra with her hair. She glanced longingly at the little black dress that hung in her closet, a gift from her friend Whitney Anderson. Whitney was the youngest sister of another of the Seattle Sharks, and was dating another of her brother's teammates. She'd told Holly that she'd cut the tags off of the brand-new dress and found out too late it didn't fit her. There was a brand-new pair of black pumps in the bag that Whitney claimed her sister Courtney didn't want, either, and just happened to be Holly's size. Whitney was a terrible liar, but Holly knew her heart was in the right place.

"You're definitely invited to my brother and sister-in-law's holiday party. The dress will be *perfect*," Whitney said. "We're going to have so much fun."

If Holly could get the night off from her other job, she'd wear the beautiful dress and shoes, but she'd be hiding out in the corner. Everyone else always seemed to have so much fun at parties. She enjoyed people-watching and eating delicious food, but she felt shy and ill-at-ease until she found some one-on-one conversation.

Holly heard her grandmother's tap at the bedroom door. "Come in," she called out.

Grandma poked her head inside Holly's room. "Honey, maybe you should put the Santa letters away before Derrick gets here," she said. "If he takes a wrong turn on the way to the men's room or something, our secret is out."

"I'll do that," Holly said.

Her grandma closed the door again as she hurried away. Holly gave the jeans and fluffy sweater on her bed a pat while she got ready to take a shower. Hopefully

Derrick knew how to drive in snow, or there might not be a date tonight at all.

DERRICK PULLED A pair of custom-made designer jeans and a medium-blue cashmere sweater out of his closet and tossed them on his bed. He'd spent the afternoon getting a tutorial on how to put chains on his Escalade from a couple of guys at the local tire shop. Snow in Alabama was an infrequent occurrence. He'd been assured repeatedly that the roads to and from the mountain passes were plowed and sanded, and he'd get where he was going safely if he took it slow and easy.

Holly must be used to the snow. He liked looking at it, and he'd enjoyed playing in it when Seattle had one of its infrequent snowstorms last year, but he talked Drew McCoy into chauffeuring him back and forth to practice until it melted. It wasn't like he could call McCoy and ask him to drive tonight; he would be at home with his wife and their baby daughter.

He heard tapping at the doorframe. "C'mon in," he called out as he grabbed a big terrycloth robe off the foot of his bed. He would walk around naked all the time if his mama and grandma weren't visiting right now.

"I'm guessing you're not going to be home for dinner," his mama said, taking a seat on the side of his bed.

"I have a date," he said.

His mama's smile was as radiant as the sun. "A date? That's wonderful. Have I met her?"

"Not yet, Mama. You will, though."

He grabbed a T-shirt and a pair of socks out of his dresser and added it to the pile on his bed. He wanted to wear the new Louis Vuitton kicks he'd bought himself the other day, but after listening to the guys at the tire shop, he'd bought a pair of sturdy snow boots this afternoon. They weren't stylish, but if he found his ass stuck somewhere, he could walk in the snow in them.

"Where did you meet her?" his mother said.

"I've talked to you about Holly before. She's the woman who works in the cafeteria at the Sharks' training camp, remember? She's little, dark-haired, freckles on her nose, and really sweet. I ran into her in the coffee shop the other day in Noel."

"The girl you liked."

"Yes, Mama." He was already getting nervous. It wasn't like he'd never invited a girl out before, but this one was special. He sat down next to his mother and turned to face her. "She's in Noel, so I'll be late getting home."

"It's snowing up there, honey."

"I'll be fine," he said. "If you and Grandma don't want to cook, order dinner and put it on my tab at Purple or Lot No. 3." One of the great benefits of living in a high-rise in moneyed downtown Bellevue was food delivery and a credit card on file at the restaurants downstairs.

"Thank you, but there's plenty of food in the refrigerator. We'll have a snack and do a little more sewing," his mother said. "Was Holly the young woman in the elf costume in the coffee shop? I saw her when we walked into the building."

He smiled at his mother. "Yes, that's her. She has to wear a costume every day to work there."

His mom reached out for his hand. Her brows knit, and she swallowed hard. "I'm a little worried about the weather, honey. Please be careful driving."

"Always, Mama," he said. He reached over to kiss her cheek. "The guys at the tire place told me it'll be just fine. I'll be back before you know it."

DERRICK SWUNG DOWN from the driver's seat of his SUV a few hours later in front of Holly's grandma's house and thanked God again that he'd had the presence of mind to order the GPS package and antiskid brake control when he'd bought his Escalade. The trip to Holly's was much longer and more treacherous than those assholes at the tire shop had led him to believe it would be. He could now say, though, he'd driven in ice and snow and lived to tell the tale.

It was snowing again. The flakes landed on his hair and his clothing. They were so soft. It was weird that something that seemed so harmless could be so dangerous.

He reached back inside the vehicle to grab the two bouquets of flowers he'd bought before leaving Bellevue and strolled up the walk to the front door. He knocked at the door and heard a woman's voice call out, "Come on in."

He stepped through the door and said, "Hello. Is Holly here?"

"Oh, yes." An older woman in brightly colored flannel pajamas, a thick terrycloth robe, and slippers got up from the couch. Her smile was warm and welcoming.

"I'm Ruth, Holly's grandma. She'll be out in a minute."

"I'm Derrick Collins," he said. He looked at the braces and bandages on Holly's grandmother's hands. "I hope you don't think I'm rude if I don't offer to shake your hand."

"Don't worry about it. I'm not shaking hands much at the moment." Ruth frowned a little as she took a good look at his earrings, but gave him a nod. "Would you like to sit down?" She indicated an overstuffed rocking chair next to the couch, and sat down once more.

Derrick extended one of the bouquets to her. "These are for you," he said.

"They're beautiful." Ruth's eyes lit up as she sniffed the bouquet. "Thank you, Derrick. It's very kind of you to bring them. I'll put them in some water, but first, let's have a little chat."

"I'd enjoy that," he said.

"Holly's living with me for the next couple of months while I recover from surgery." She held up her hands, and he nodded. "Her parents live in Arizona. I know they'd want me to impress on you how important their daughter is to them, and that they would expect you to act like a gentleman during your date."

"Of course, ma'am," he said.

"I've seen your on-field antics, Mr. Collins, and I've read a few things on the sports page that leave me a bit concerned."

She was probably referring to his sack dance, which had been called "the baby-making dance" by more than one sports commentator. She might have also read a few things about his previous relationships, but he wasn't bringing those up. No need to borrow trouble.

"I'm not like that when I'm not playing—"

She interrupted him before he could finish his sentence. "You also realize that Holly has to be at work at five AM tomorrow morning."

"Then I will bring her home by nine o'clock," Derrick said.

He was a little shocked at Holly's grandma's comments, but he did his best not to show it. Maybe Holly had a change of heart in the past twenty-four hours and really didn't want to go out with him after all. Did she put her grandma up to this? Maybe she didn't like men who wore earrings. Two-carat diamond studs in each earlobe might be a bit over the top.

He heard light footsteps behind him, and Holly walked into the room. She looked amazing in a pair of jeans and a light-blue fluffy sweater that brought out her blue eyes. A few tendrils of dark hair curled around her face. He got to his feet.

"I'm sorry it took me a few minutes," she said. "I... I had to take care of something." He saw a flush spread over her cheekbones. In other words, she'd probably changed her clothes a few times. She reached out to give him a hug. "It's nice to see you."

Her warm greeting put him at ease. She wanted to spend some time with him too. She probably hadn't been counting the minutes like he had, but he'd take what he could get from this girl.

"It's great to see you too."

He presented Holly with the second bouquet, and she beamed. He'd bring her flowers every day if he could see that radiant smile. If he didn't know any better, he'd say he'd been kicked in the ass by love or some pretty intense infatuation. She was just so *cute* standing there, and he couldn't stop staring at her. He noted she was also wearing a pair of snow boots; at least those guys at the tire shop hadn't steered him wrong on *that* one.

If he moved his ass, he'd get to spend a couple of hours chatting with her.

"You brought my grandma flowers? Oh, that is so sweet. Grandma, let me put these into water before I go." She reached out for her grandma's bouquet and turned to vanish into what he imagined was the kitchen.

He fidgeted. Most of the women he'd dated lived with roommates who either ignored his arrival for a date or tried to get a date with him themselves. Holly's grandma's scrutiny left him a little freaked out.

"Have you been to the Mexican restaurant here?" he asked Ruth.

"Yes, I have," she said. "It's pretty good, but we go to the pizza place more often. It's two blocks away. It's also a little quieter and better for conversation." He could have sworn Ruth winked at him. "How do you feel about pizza?"

"I'm a fan. You've sold me," he said. He thought for a moment. "Would you like us to bring you something to eat on our way home?"

Holly's grandma's formerly stern expression melted into a smile. "I don't want to inconvenience you."

"I wouldn't offer if it was a problem. We'll call you before we head back home and pick up what you want."

Fifteen minutes later, he'd helped Holly into her winter coat, scarf, and stocking hat, and they stepped outside.

"Would you like to walk to the pizza place?" he asked Holly. "Your grandma talked me out of the Mexican food."

She let out a laugh. "She likes the pizza place better, so I'm not surprised by that. A walk might be nice."

The snow was falling faster, and a brisk wind blew the flakes into their faces. He held out his arm for her to slide her hand through as they walked.

"It wasn't snowing when I got home earlier," she said. "I hope this doesn't mean we're getting another big storm."

"Maybe it'll slow down while we're having dinner," he said.

The clouds thickening overhead, though, weren't comforting. He saw a car sliding a bit on the ice and freshly fallen snow as the driver made his way down Noel's main street, and he reached out to make sure Holly walked on the interior of the sidewalk next to him. She grinned up at him.

"You're going to stop the car if it skids onto the sidewalk?" she teased.

"I'll block it back into the other lane for you," he said.

They turned onto the street leading to the pizza place, and he reached out for her hand. Despite the thick mittens she wore, her hand was warm and small inside his. He curled his fingers protectively around it. A few more steps, and they'd be inside again. He saw more cars sliding on the street a few hundred feet ahead of them. Maybe they were just really bad drivers.

Holly glanced up at him again. Maybe it was his imagination, but she clutched his hand a little more tightly. He felt ten feet tall as a result.

"We'll be okay," he reassured her. He increased his stride. "They're nowhere near us."

The restaurant was deserted. The guy behind the counter called out, "Hey, Holly. You didn't call ahead this time."

"We're dining in," she said. She reached up to pull off her hat and her scarf. A few strands of hair clung to her cold-reddened cheeks. Derrick wondered if she'd be shocked if he kissed her. Right now.

The guy behind the counter stared at Derrick.

Holly said, "We're seating ourselves tonight, aren't we?" She sat down at a table for two, and Derrick pulled a twenty out of his money clip and slid it on the counter.

"There's twenty bucks in it for you if you don't call or text all your friends and tell them I'm here right now," he said to the kid.

"I would have settled for an autograph," the kid told him.

"Well, then. I'll make sure you get one of those too." Derrick reached out to fist-bump with the kid. "Will you bring us whatever it is Holly likes to drink, and bring me a Coke, please?"

Derrick jammed the twenty into the tip jar in front of the cash register and returned to the table.

The counter guy brought a large Coke for Derrick, a glass of white wine for Holly, and a couple of laminated menus.

"Does your grandma still like the chop-chop salad? I'll make sure there's one for her when you're ready to leave," the server said. "You probably heard the pass is closed in both directions."

Oh, shit, Derrick thought. The passes were the only way back over the mountains, and he'd taken the pass that was typically the easiest to navigate during winter weather.

He also needed to be at the practice facility by eight AM tomorrow morning.

"What? No. Really?" Holly said. "When?"

"It was just on the radio. Several jackknifed semis and an avalanche, plus another huge storm is on its way. Nobody's getting out of town until tomorrow morning at the earliest." He pulled an order pad out of his pocket. "What would you like?"

Derrick's coach was going to kill him if he wasn't at practice tomorrow. The Sharks were playing Denver on Sunday afternoon. Hopefully he'd be out of Noel by then. The tire guys hadn't said a word about this possibility, either.

"You're not going to be able to get out of here tonight," Holly said to him. "This isn't good."

"Let's worry about that later," Derrick said.

Chapter Four

HOLLY HAD BEEN shy all of her life. She was just fine when she was at work or school; she could manage to overcome her bashfulness long enough to talk with customers or ask her fellow students questions. Talking with members of the opposite sex she was interested in, though, was a whole other story. She was tongue-tied. She blushed herself into a coma. Most of the time she all but ran away; she envied other women who could talk and flirt easily with someone they were interested in. She wished she could be like them.

Dating was a special kind of torture. She was bad at small talk. Plus, it was important to be a fun person on a date, or the person you were out with might decide he didn't want a second date.

Holly had lost her heart to Derrick—and his impish grin—two years ago in the Sharks' cafeteria's breakfast line. He teased her and talked with her whenever he saw her, but she told herself that he joked around with everyone. She wasn't special.

She still couldn't believe he'd asked her out. She was going to have to make an extra effort tonight.

"How's the pizza?" he asked her.

"It's...it's good," she said.

"Would you like something else to eat instead? You've only had a couple of bites."

She felt her face getting hot. "I'm not very hungry," she said. It was hard to eat when her stomach was full of butterflies.

He leaned across the table toward her and reached out to take her hand in his. Her heart felt like it would beat its way out of her chest. She was sure her palms were sweaty. He didn't seem to mind. He looked into her eyes.

"It's just me, Holly," he said. His dark eyes softened like chocolate in summertime. "I want to get to know you. Talk to me." The huge diamond studs in his ears sparkled in the dimly lit restaurant.

She nodded and swallowed hard. He stroked her hand with his thumb—a slow, deliberate movement across her skin.

"You feel shy around me," he said.

Her voice sounded like the creak of a rusty hinge. "Yes."

His smile was dazzling. He was still stroking her hand, and she felt him grip it a little more tightly in his. "Here's an idea, then. Close your eyes."

"Excuse me?"

His laugh bounced around the quiet restaurant. "Let's see if it works. Try it. I'll make sure you're safe. Take a deep breath too."

His suggestion sounded a little weird to her, but it was worth a try. She closed her eyes. She felt him lean closer to her. He smelled like clean skin and a whiff of what she imagined must have been very expensive men's cologne. "So, Holly. Have you lived in Noel for a while?"

"I don't really live here," she said. "I'm staying with my grandma until she's feeling better. I have an apartment with two of Zach Anderson's sisters. I'll be back there before school starts again."

"What's your major?"

"Nursing."

"Ahhh," he said. "That's good. You'll be able to fix me right up after a game, then."

Little did he know, she'd be thrilled to. She pulled in another breath. Surprisingly enough, closing her eyes while they talked seemed to help with her nervousness.

"Don't the trainers do that stuff?" she said.

"They're not as pretty as you are."

She could feel her face getting warm again, and she opened her eyes a little.

"Uh-uh. Can't look at me right now," he said. "You're going to remember you're feeling shy, and you'll stop talking to me."

She closed her eyes. He reached out with his other hand to touch her jawline with his fingertips.

"That's better. I could ask you a lot of questions about your family and your interests, and I'm getting to them all, but there's one question I'd really like to know the answer to." He was now holding her hand with both of his. He was still stroking her skin with one thumb. Her heart skipped a beat as adrenaline surged through her. "You were crying when I walked into the coffee shop the other day. What's wrong? Is there anything I can do to help?"

Only a few members of Noel's Merchants' Association knew "Santa's" true identity. Her grandma had made Holly vow to keep the thirty-year-old secret. If it got out that someone in Noel had been answering the letters all these years, it would crush the hopes of countless local children. On top of that, Holly's grandmother didn't want anyone else to find out she'd enlisted Holly's help this year, either.

"It's not that big of a deal," she said.

"It is to me," he said. "Tell me all about it."

She swallowed hard. He was going to persist, and she had to tell him something. It wasn't like she was lying to him if she made up a few of the details. She didn't want to betray her grandma's secret. She thought for a few seconds.

"I was reading one of those stories people post on Facebook. You know, some little boy wrote to Santa Claus and asked Santa to bring toys for his younger brother and sister and a job for his mom, but didn't ask for anything for himself."

"Was he local?" Derrick said.

"I don't think so," she said. "I…I was tired, and I got choked up. It's silly."

"No, it's not," he said. "You're tenderhearted."

She bowed her head a bit. The fact that she temporarily couldn't see heightened all of her other senses, and she felt the air move and his body heat as he leaned closer to her. "Too sentimental," she said.

"No such thing." He reached out to stroke her cheek again. "The kid's community must be getting together to help him and his family out."

"I think so," she said. She was uncomfortable with shading the truth, but it wasn't her secret to share. Maybe she should change the subject instead. "Is it still snowing outside?"

"Yes, and it looks like it's coming down faster."

She didn't hear the usual traffic noise outside of Noel Pizza, which was located on the main drag through the small town. The sidewalk outside the little restaurant was typically crowded with tourists and locals. She didn't hear any of the usual laughter and music from Noel's main street, either. In other words the storm was bad, and Derrick wasn't getting out of there anytime soon.

She was torn between concern that he might be stuck for a while, and happiness that she could spend a little more time with him. "Maybe I should take a look outside at the weather. Grandma's going to worry."

"We'll be fine," he soothed. "Do you want to call her?"

"I should. Plus, she's probably hungry by now."

Holly heard the rumble of Derrick's laughter. "I'll make sure she gets some food. What's her number?"

She recited the number from memory, and he put his now-ringing phone into her free hand.

"Hello?"

"Grandma, it's me. We're still at the pizza place. Want me to bring you some salad?"

"I'd like that, but you need to come home right now. There's a bigger storm right behind this one. Both of the inns in town are full, too," Grandma said. "Derrick's welcome overnight here."

"We'll be home in a few minutes, Grandma. We'll be careful." She opened her eyes, hit "end," and handed the phone back to him. Storm or no, the thought of Derrick's staying overnight left her a little breathless with excitement. "She said there's another storm coming, everywhere you could stay is full, and you have an invitation to spend the night at our house."

OVERNIGHT, HUH? PERFECT. Derrick was going to have to fork over thousands in fines for missing practice tomorrow—and deal with the ration of shit his teammates were going to subject him to when they found out he'd driven a hundred miles one way in a snowstorm to go on a date—but the prospect of spending more time with her warmed his heart.

"That's nice of your grandma to invite me," he said. "I was wondering for a few minutes there if I needed to ask the pizza guys if they had a back room and a cot."

"Oh, no," she said. "Y-you can sleep in my room. I'll sleep on the couch." Her face flushed bright red, and he almost laughed aloud.

"Oh, no, Holly. My mama would smack me, and so would my grandma. They taught me better than that. I'll be very comfortable on the couch tonight, and thank you for the offer."

She was still blushing and her eyes sparkled. He watched her mouth twitch into a smile. She had to get up early tomorrow morning to go to work, but he wondered how much sleep they were actually going to get. He wasn't making his move in Holly's grandma's house, but the thought of her only a few feet away from him might make for a pretty sleepless night.

Maybe he should try to get home later on. The passes couldn't be closed forever, could they? He had to get to his job in the morning. His coach was fair, but he didn't tolerate lateness or absenteeism during the season. At all.

Holly excused herself to visit the ladies' room, and Derrick pulled up weather.com on his phone. It might have been nice if he'd checked things before he left Bellevue, but he was so impatient to see Holly again that he hadn't bothered to glance at the current conditions in the mountains that bracketed the Seattle area. He'd been told it might snow, but between his Escalade and his brand-new snow boots, he'd thought it wasn't that big of a deal. He was pretty shocked at the red-flagged weather "warnings" of multiple snowstorms and the advisory to stay off the roads until at least six o'clock tomorrow morning. In other words, the storms were more severe than he'd imagined, and he was a dumbass for not double-checking.

Holly hadn't arrived back at the table yet, so he texted his mama and his teammate Drew McCoy: I'M SAFE. STUCK IN NOEL. WILL CALL YOU TOMORROW MORNING.

Twenty minutes later, Derrick had ordered additional food for Holly and her grandma to carry out. He'd also settled up with the pizza guy on both the autograph he'd promised and the bill. He hefted two shopping bags full of food and beverages while Holly clung to his arm. The pizza guys flipped the "closed" sign over and locked the front doors behind them.

The weather conditions had deteriorated significantly in the hour and a half or so since they'd walked to the pizza place. Derrick was glad Holly knew where she was going. He wouldn't have had any idea how to get her back home in near white-out conditions. Packed ice and snow crunched under their feet. The blowing snow smacked them in the face.

He wondered if they could move faster if he carried her.

She pulled him around the corner and onto the street where her grandmother lived. There wasn't a car on the road right now. He saw the glimmer of light from the houses on either side of the street, but he couldn't see details. The only sounds that registered was the howling of the wind.

"Does it snow like this all the time?" he asked her.

"What?" she said.

He put his mouth closer to her ear. "Where's your grandma's house?"

"Halfway up the block."

They were both bent almost double against the swirling wind and snow. Every step was an effort for him. He couldn't imagine how she could stand up in this. He dropped her hand and reached around her waist to pull her into his side. If they couldn't make it to her grandma's house, they'd freeze to death out here.

"Come on, Holly," he shouted. "We're almost there."

He felt her arms wrap around him. "Three more houses," she shouted back.

He kept moving forward. The top of her stocking cap tickled his chin. He saw a porch light up ahead through the whirling snow and hoped it was her grandma's house. Holly tugged him forward and did her best to stay upright.

Mercifully the porch light did belong to Holly's grandma's house. They fought their way up the front steps, and Holly tried to grip the doorknob in one shivering hand.

"Let me do it," he said. He swung the front door open, ushered her in, and slammed the door behind him. A burst of snowflakes followed them inside.

Holly's grandma was already off the couch and hurrying over to them. "I was ready to call the police." She reached out to wrap her arms around Holly. "You're shivering. Come in here where it's warm."

"It's so cold," Holly managed to get out.

Derrick was cold, too, but not like she was. He'd been so busy trying to get her to talk to him he hadn't even noticed the weather. He couldn't believe that a two-block walk had turned into a life-or-death situation that fast, either.

Holly's grandmother helped her pull off her coat, hat, and gloves while nudging her closer to an iron stove in one corner of the family room. "Derrick," she called out. "Come on in here. You must be freezing."

"It's my fault we weren't home sooner," he said to Ruth. "Is she okay?"

"She'll be fine," Holly's grandmother said. "Honey, why didn't you leave when you saw it was getting so bad outside?"

"We were talking and I...I..." Despite the fact Holly was obviously cold, she pulled Derrick closer to the iron stove. "It's my fault, Grandma," she said. "Don't be mad at him."

The lights in the house flickered.

Chapter Five

HOLLY FINALLY STOPPED shivering a few minutes later, but she wondered if she'd just jumped out of the frying pan and into the fire. The differences between her life and Derrick Collins's could not have been more glaring. He'd pulled off brand-new, expensive hiking boots inside her grandma's front door, and then dropped an equally expensive—and equally brand-new—North Face jacket next to them. They landed on the threadbare carpeting that covered the floors of Grandma's manufactured home. He still wore what she was sure was a cashmere scarf around his neck as he sat on the worn couch in the family room, which was covered in old blankets.

Grandma managed to make enough to live on from her little yarn shop, but luxuries like new furniture and updated decorating weren't in her budget. Holly had stayed with her grandma plenty of times over the years, and neither of them minded their humble surroundings.

It was home. They had enough to eat, a roof over their heads, and bought clothes and other necessities at a thrift shop in Wenatchee. They squeezed out a little extra to get pizza once in a while or maybe see a movie at the teeny theater in town that showed classic films. Holly was also paying her grandma rent while she was here, despite the fact Grandma had refused the money repeatedly. It would help Grandma pay the electric bills.

Speaking of electric bills, after some pretty intense flickering, the lights and the electric heat thankfully stayed on. Wait until Derrick found out that they didn't have cable TV, either, Holly thought.

She'd make more money when she graduated from nursing school and got a job, but she wondered if the years of making every cent last as long as possible would stick with her. Saving money was never a bad thing. She was currently in a house, however, with a man whose annual salary was more than both she and Grandma would see in a lifetime.

The less-than-fancy surroundings didn't seem to bother him. "Is it okay if I put my feet up?" he said to her grandma before using the (worn) footstool in front of the couch.

"Of course it is. Make yourself at home," Grandma said. "Would you like something to drink, Derrick?" She nodded toward the kitchen. "I can put the kettle on. We have tea, cocoa, or I could make some coffee if you'd like."

"Thank you," he said. "I'd actually love a glass of water, please."

"Coming right up," Holly said.

She escaped to the kitchen. Shabby chic was in fashion, but Grandma's home was just "shabby." It was clean, however. She grabbed a glass out of the cabinet next to the kitchen sink and filled it with fresh water. Her grandma had put the food Derrick brought into the refrigerator already. She was supposed to be relaxing, but she was in the other room fussing over Derrick instead.

"Why don't you sit down and relax, Miss Ruth?" she heard Derrick say. "I'll go get that salad we brought you. Maybe Holly can help me find a bowl to put it in too."

"I can get it," she heard her grandma insist.

"Oh, no. You have a seat. I'll be back in two shakes of a lamb's tail." Derrick rounded the kitchen door and grinned at Holly. "Your grandma needs some salad."

Holly pulled the to-go container out of the refrigerator, grabbed a fork out of the drawer, and put them down on the kitchen counter. She handed him the glass of water he'd asked for. "Do you need anything else right now?"

"I'm good," he said. "Then again, there's something I forgot."

"What do you need? Maybe I can help."

He moved closer to her, and she tipped her head back to look up at him. He reached out to cup one of her cheeks in his big hand. "I had a great time tonight. Thanks for having pizza with me."

"I had a nice time too. Th-thank you for inviting me," she stammered. There was so much more she'd like to say, but she was tongue-tied again. He was moving closer to her, and he reached out to put his drinking glass down on the counter.

"Maybe we could try this again when we're not in the middle of a snowstorm," he said. "I'd like a second date."

She started nodding like one of those bobbleheads, and forced herself to stop before he thought she was even more of a dork.

"Yes. I...Yes, I would too. I...that would be fun."

He took another half-step toward her. She did her best to pull in a breath.

"Normally, I would have kissed you good night at your front door, but getting us inside before we froze to death seemed like the best thing to do right then," he said.

"Oh, yes. Absolutely. I—"

He reached out, slid his arms around her waist, and pulled her close. "I don't want to disrespect your grandma's wishes," he softly said. "She said I needed to treat you like a lady."

Holly almost let out a groan. She loved Grandma, but they needed to have a little chat later. "Sorry," she whispered.

He grinned at her. "I promise I'll behave myself, unless you don't want me to." She couldn't help it; she laughed. "Plus," he continued, "she said you have to be up very early in the morning to go to work, so we'll have to say good night."

Maybe she didn't need sleep. One thing's for sure, she had no interest in stepping away from him right now. He surrounded her, and she wanted to stay in his arms. Her heart was beating double-time, the blood was effervescent in her veins, and she summoned the nerve to move a little closer to him as she let out a happy sigh.

He kissed her cheek, and laid his scratchier one against hers. A few seconds later, she slid her arms around his neck too. "Good night, sweet Holly. Thanks for saving me from the snowstorm."

She had to laugh a little. "I think you saved *me*."

"We'll figure out who saved who later," he said. She felt his deep voice vibrating through her. She wished he'd kiss her again. Maybe she should kiss *him*.

He must have read her mind. He took her face in both of his hands. "Don't tell your grandma," he whispered. His breath was warm on her cheek.

"Tell her what?"

"I'm going to kiss you."

Her head was bobbing around as she frantically nodded yes. She probably looked ridiculous, but he didn't seem to care. Her eyelids fluttered closed as his mouth touched hers, sweet and soft. It wasn't a long kiss, but she knew she'd never forget it. She felt the zing at his tender touch from the top of her head to her toes.

"A little more?" he asked.

"Oh, yes."

His arms wrapped around her again, and he slowly traced her lips with his tongue. It slid into her mouth. He tasted like the peppermints Noel Pizza kept in a jar on the front counter. They explored each other for a while as quietly as possible, but maybe not quietly enough.

"Holly, honey," her grandma called out from the family room. Holly was *absolutely* going to have a conversation with Grandma when Derrick was out of earshot, and she stifled a groan. All they were doing was a little kissing. He rested one big hand on her butt, which she enjoyed. "Would you please bring me some salad?"

Derrick let out a snort. "I'll get it for you, Miss Ruth," he said loudly enough for her grandma to hear.

"She's onto us," Holly said softly.

"Damn right." He grinned at her. "I'll see you tomorrow morning." His voice dropped. "We're *definitely* kissing on the second date."

"I'll look forward to that." She tried to pull in a breath. Her head was spinning. She couldn't have stopped smiling if her life depended on it. "Are you sure you don't want to stay in my room instead? You need a good night's sleep. Don't you have to go to practice?"

"I'm sure your room is very comfortable, but I'll be fine out here. Sweet dreams," he said.

She felt him kiss the top of her head as he held her. She took a deep breath of his scent: clean skin, a whiff of expensive cologne, and freshly pressed clothes. "You, too," she whispered. She reached up to kiss his cheek. "Good night."

Fifteen minutes later she was ready for bed, and she slid between flannel sheets. She set her alarm for four AM. Hopefully the wind still blowing snow against her window would stop, and the streets would be plowed enough for her to walk the three blocks to Caffeine Addiction in the morning.

She could hear her grandma's voice in the family room, and Derrick's much deeper one. She wanted to hear what they were talking about, but she concentrated on calming breaths as she waited for sleep to come.

He'd asked her out again. She couldn't remember the last time she was this excited.

AN HOUR OR SO later, Derrick cleared the dirty dishes off of the family room coffee table, got to his feet, and said, "Is there anything else I could get for you from the kitchen, Miss Ruth?"

"Oh, no," she said. "You don't have to do that. I can clean up."

"Absolutely not," he teased. "You relax. I'll be back in a few minutes."

Holly's grandma had forgotten her earlier reserve about him, and told him story after story about her granddaughter. Her obvious pride in Holly's hard work and perseverance, and her love for her granddaughter, warmed his heart. He knew his mama and grandma bragged about him too. He wasn't perfect by any stretch of the imagination, but they seemed to think he was.

He hoped he could live up to the person his loved ones believed him to be. He wondered if he could do anything in his life comparable to the brave actions of his grandpa, who'd fought in World War II and marched with Martin Luther King. Derrick's dad had served his country, too, and Derrick's brother, Trevon, was still in Afghanistan. Playing in the NFL was a pretty big deal, but he wanted to make his mark on the world as well.

He loaded the few dirty dishes into the dishwasher and returned to the family room to find Holly's grandmother drowsing in her big chair. He reached out for one of the blankets Holly had brought him before she went to bed and carefully spread it over her grandma.

"Good night, Miss Ruth."

Her only response was a soft snore. He grinned to himself and grabbed the TV remote. If he kept it down, hopefully she'd get some good rest.

It had been years since he'd encountered a noncable TV set. He settled on a grainy news broadcast from Seattle and pulled some more of the blankets around himself. According to the newscasters, he wasn't getting out of here anytime soon. The passes were closed due to white-out conditions and resulting avalanches. They wouldn't reopen until the snow stopped falling. He fumbled in his pocket for his cell phone, and got up from the couch to approach the living room window.

Two bars. He'd better text McCoy and Taylor and tell them he was stuck. He'd call his coach too. Just thinking about explaining why he was a hundred miles from home right now made him stifle a groan. If he couldn't get coverage, though, he couldn't call anyone at all. Maybe the cell coverage was better elsewhere in the house. He'd try the kitchen first; there was a window in there. A couple more bars popped up as he got closer to the window. Thank God.

His mother's cell phone rang once before he heard her voice. "Derrick Luther Collins, where are you?"

"Didn't you get my text, Mama?"

"That would be a 'no,'" his mother said.

He did his best to keep his voice down. "I'm staying overnight at Holly's grandma's house because it's all snowed in. I'm fine. I'll be home as soon as I can."

"We were so scared, young man—"

"I know, Mama. I'm sorry I haven't called before now. I'll call you in the morning when I can get my phone charger out of my rig."

"I'll tell your grandma you're fine."

"Thanks, Mama. See you tomorrow," he said.

He heard footsteps behind him, and Holly's grandma appeared at the kitchen door. She was rubbing her eyes.

"I'm going to bed, Derrick. Do you need anything else?" she asked.

"No, thank you. Is there anything you need—some water, or something to eat?"

"I'm fine." She shuffled over to him, and got on her tip-toes to kiss his cheek. "Sleep well. See you in the morning."

"You, too," he said.

Fifteen minutes later, Derrick spread an old sheet over Miss Ruth's family room floor. He gave up trying to sleep on the couch when more of him hung off it than on it. He curled into the blankets and stared at the ceiling. He was going to get one hell of a fine—and a legendary tongue-lashing at the least—for missing practice tomorrow, but he couldn't seem to work up the usual sense of urgency about the fact that the Sharks were fighting for their lives in the playoff picture right now. He'd be damned if the Miners went to the big game again. Right now, though, he couldn't stop thinking about Holly. He remembered her shy smiles, the way she fit against him, and the soft-ness of her skin. He also remembered the butterflies in his stomach whenever she was near. She was a curvy little thing too. He'd always loved a woman with some flesh on her bones. She probably thought her butt was too big, and that he didn't like the slight roll over the top of her jeans. She'd be wrong.

She wouldn't demand that he take her to the most exclusive nightclubs or ask for his help establishing her singing or modeling career. She worked hard to prepare for and establish a career that would have her helping others every day. If all that wasn't enough, his mama and his grandma were going to love her too.

It took a little coaxing to get her to talk with him, but it was worth the effort. He could remember how she smelled, too: a combination of powder, soft floral perfume, and freshly washed cotton. She was so shy with him at first, but the way she snuggled against him with perfect confidence made him wish they were alone.

Her grandma would *not* be happy if she could read his mind right now.

The pizza place was fine, but he'd love to take Holly someplace elegant for dinner. They could go dancing too. He couldn't wait to spend more time with her.

He was still tossing and turning an hour later. Maybe he could get some sleep if he had another glass of water. He pulled himself off of the living room floor and padded into the kitchen. The light over the oven was still on, and he grabbed the drinking glass he'd used earlier. He glanced out of the window over the sink. The storm hadn't let up at all.

Damn.

A kitchen table and four chairs sat in an alcove a few feet away. He strolled over, pulled a chair out and parked it while he drank his water.

The table was covered with mail. Letters stamped and ready to mail sat in a small pile on his left. He glanced at the return address:

Santa Claus
North Pole

"What the hell?" he muttered to himself.

Unopened letters sat in a stack on the other side of the table. Directly in front of him a letter with no return address, written on notebook paper, rested on the table next to a spiral notebook. He knew he shouldn't be snooping in someone else's private business, but he read the letter. It was from a kid asking for presents for his little sister and brother and a job for his mom for Christmas, just like the letter Holly had been crying over yesterday.

Two minutes later, he dug beneath the letter to discover a plain envelope addressed to "Santa Claus, North Pole" in the same messy printing. He was going to find this Michael kid and his family if it was the last thing he ever did.

Somebody in this house was playing Santa Claus, and he wanted in on the action.

Chapter Six

HOLLY'S ALARM WENT off much too early the next morning, and she let out a quiet groan in her darkened bedroom. She could hear the wind, still howling outside. She forced herself to sit up against the headboard as she grabbed her cell phone off of the nightstand. She stared at the blinking message light for a few seconds. Unless she was seeing things, someone had tried to call her last night. She hit the voicemail button on the phone, and she pulled the blankets around herself a bit more when she heard her boss's voice.

"Holly, the power's out on Main Street. We can't open until it's back on, and the power company can't fix it until the storm lets up a little." She heard him sigh. "Get some extra sleep, and I'll call you later."

The good news: She didn't have to crawl out of bed right now. The bad news: Missing the hours was money out of her pocket. The other bad news: the Noel

Merchants' Association was having a holiday gathering tonight, and Holly was one of the servers for the caterer doing the event. If things didn't improve on the weather front, she'd be out an entire day's pay.

She shoved the phone onto her nightstand, flopped into her pillows, and yanked the blankets over her head. She didn't want to be freaking out over money at 4:06 AM. She wanted to be thinking about the fact that the guy she'd had a crush on for two years now was (hopefully) asleep on her grandma's family room couch.

Maybe she should go and check on him, if she had nothing better to do than lie there and flip out over things she couldn't change. She shoved herself out of the blankets and grabbed the less-than-stylish, worn bathrobe she'd left at the foot of her bed the night before. Grandma's iron stove might be out of fuel too. She turned the thermostat way down at night to save money. Derrick was going to freeze his butt off if she didn't make sure the stove was still heating the house.

Holly wrapped the robe around herself as she dashed across the hall to make a pit stop. She twisted her long hair into a coil of sorts and pulled it off of her neck with a banana clip. If she took a shower, did something with her hair, and put on a little makeup, she'd wake up everyone in the house. She could only hope that if Derrick saw her like this he didn't scream and run.

She padded down the hallway and into the family room. Someone had left the kitchen light on during the night; she could at least see where she was going as a result.

Grandma's family room was a rectangle shape. Between the couch and chair and Derrick, there wasn't a lot of room to maneuver. He'd shoved the coffee table that usually sat in front of the couch against the far wall to give himself a bit more room.

Derrick was sprawled out on the family room floor, hugging a pillow, and naked from the waist up. He was snoring. It wasn't a delicate thing, but she smiled a little. She wondered if the sound had lulled her grandma to sleep last night. Grandma had mentioned several times before that Grandpa's snoring had never bothered her, and that she still missed it—and him.

She smiled at the sunburst tattoo on Derrick's shoulder. She peeked around the corner once more, and he didn't stir. The iron stove was out of fuel.

Right now, she couldn't get through the family room without either stepping on Derrick or waking him up. A few minutes later, he rolled over onto one side, effectively clearing a nice path for her to get through the family room without disturbing him. She added pellets to the stove as quietly as possible. He stirred a little, but he didn't wake up. She waited until she'd tiptoed back out of the family room before letting out a sigh of relief.

She knew she wasn't going to be able to go back to sleep. Maybe she should find something to do for a couple of hours while Derrick slept. She made her way into the kitchen.

Her heart dropped as she surveyed the kitchen table. Her carefully arranged pile of opened letters was a bit messed up. An empty drinking glass sat next to them

on the table. She moved closer. A folded-in-half piece
of spiral notebook paper lay next to the letters. The note
read:

> Holly,
>> Whatever you're doing with this, I want in.
>> Derrick

She'd forgotten to put the letters away like Grandma
asked before she went out with Derrick last night, and
now she saw evidence that he had read at least one. The
envelope to Michael's letter lay on top of the smudged
piece of notebook paper. She got up from the table and
grabbed a cloth shopping bag for the already-stamped
answers to go to the post office as soon as it quit snowing.

She had nobody to blame but herself for his having
read at least one of the letters.

She sat down at the table and got to work, making
notes on places she could start looking for Michael and
his family. The printing on Michael's letter looked more
like a junior high student's than a child in elementary
school; she could call the principal later today. Noel's
Santa Claus was a friendly, retired gentleman who'd been
doing the job for twenty years now. The kids who had
come to see him in previous years were now bringing
their own kids, and he remembered them all. The owner
of Noel's candy shop knew a lot of local children too.
There had to be more places that kids hung out in this
town besides the playground in the town square. She'd
ask her grandma later if she had any more ideas.

Holly was so intent on responding to a letter from a young lady who had asked for a new American Girl doll, and clothes for the doll, from Santa that she didn't hear Derrick's footsteps until he walked into the kitchen. He was wearing the jeans he'd worn last night, and carried his scrunched-up T-shirt in one big fist. He pulled out the chair next to her, dropped into it, and regarded her with sleepy eyes.

"Hey," he said.

"Good morning."

Holly nudged the bag with the other letters under the opposite kitchen chair with one foot. She tried not to stare at his bare chest. It was a losing battle.

"Is there coffee?" he asked. He folded his arms on the table and laid his head on them. "Shit, I'm tired."

"I'll make you some," she told him as she got up from the table to switch on the coffee pot.

"Mornings suck," he groaned. "I fuc—flippin' hate them."

She turned away from him so he wouldn't see her smile. He had the presence of mind to remember he was in someone else's house, and her grandma might not appreciate a big, half-naked male wandering around, spouting the f-bomb at full volume before six AM. She remembered that Derrick didn't care for waking up early from training camp. He was always sweet to her, but his teammates gave him a wide berth until he had at least one cup of coffee. She also remembered an interesting incident in which it looked like he and Drew McCoy were about to kill each other in the food line, so she decided that maybe she should hurry up with the coffee.

A few minutes later, the blessed sounds and scent of percolating coffee wafted through her grandma's kitchen, and she took a look inside of the refrigerator to figure out what she could make for breakfast. Derrick was still head-down on the kitchen table and dozing. Hopefully, he wouldn't drool on the letters, or even worse, try to read them.

"Derrick," she said. "Do you want to go sleep in my room for a couple of hours?"

"With you? I accept," he said.

She burst out laughing. He managed a grin in return.

"I'm fine," he mumbled. "Is there breakfast?"

"I'll have to make some."

"Do you have a cell phone charger? Mine's in the Escalade." He sat up and rubbed his eyes. "Maybe I should stop being such a chickenshit and go get it," he muttered. "It's colder than a well digger's ass out there." He pulled his T-shirt on.

Holly was pretty used to the Sharks and language that would make most people want to wash Derrick's mouth out with soap. Her grandma would probably pretend to be appalled and chuckle about it later.

The storm was still blowing snow against the kitchen window. It was too dark outside to see how deep it had gotten overnight, but the fact Holly still hadn't heard a car pass Grandma's house this morning told her that it was a lot worse than he knew out there.

"My charger may not work with your phone," she said. "I still have a regular phone. You know, the kind that doesn't get e-mails or anything."

His lips turned up in a smile. "You're the only one left," he said.

"Maybe. I'll go get it, and we'll see if it works. Why don't you think of what sounds good for breakfast in the meantime?" Holly grabbed the charger out of her purse and returned to the kitchen to find Derrick rummaging around in the refrigerator.

"Cold pizza works just fine," he said, grabbing a slice of one of the pies he'd brought back to Grandma's house. "You want some?"

"I'll heat yours up if you'd like," she said.

"Don't worry about it. I lived on cold pizza in college." He took a huge bite, sat down at the table again, and chewed for a minute or two. "Aren't you supposed to go to work this morning?"

"My boss called me earlier and told me to stay home. There's no power on Main Street." She pulled the phone out of her bathrobe pocket to take a look for any missed calls. "It must not be back on yet."

"Good. You can spend the day with me," he said.

DERRICK WAS STILL a bit pissed off at the world. He hated mornings. So far, however, this one wasn't bad. Holly was all smiles, compared to his grumpiness. He knew she had to be exhausted, but she was doing her best to make sure he was comfortable. Maybe he should get his ass off of the chair and see what he could do to help her.

She arrived back in the kitchen with her phone charger and put it down on the counter while she grabbed a couple of mugs out of the cupboard over the sink. "If your phone doesn't fit it, you can use mine to make calls if you'd like. Do you want milk or sugar in your coffee?"

"Neither," he said. He waited for her to bring the mugs, the half-gallon of milk, and the coffee carafe to the table. She poured a mugful for him, put it down in front of him, and said, "Is there anything else you need right now?"

"You're waiting on me just like you did at the Sharks' cafeteria," he teased. "You always take good care of me, girl."

Her smile was bashful. "I can't help it," she said.

"I like it," he said. He reached out to squeeze her hand. She squeezed back, and his heart went ba-bump in his chest. He might actually enjoy waking up in the mornings if Holly was with him.

His thoughts turned to the pile of letters on the table. He should wait until later to bring them up. Maybe he should talk with her about them when he wasn't quite so cranky still. He took a cautious sip of the coffee. It was still too hot.

"Yeah, there is one more thing. Where'd you get these letters to Santa Claus?" he asked, nodding at the small stack still on the kitchen table.

HOLLY GOT UP from the table, opened the refrigerator, and grabbed one of the pizza boxes inside. She placed a few slices on a cookie sheet and put it in the oven to warm.

It might be a good idea to face this conversation with a bit more than coffee in her now-churning stomach.

She'd forgotten to put the letters away last night like her grandma asked her to, and now she was going to have to invent yet another story to cover up. She did her best not to lie as a rule, but this was a pretty big secret to entrust to someone she wasn't sure could keep it.

"Holly?" he said.

"I'll be with you in a moment."

"That doesn't answer my question."

She walked back to the table on now-leaden legs and sank into the chair. He didn't take his eyes off of hers. The only noises in the room were their breathing and the wind that was still whipping around outside. Seconds later, her cell phone rang. She grabbed it out of her pocket. Her boss's number was on the screen.

"Holly, sorry to bother you again. We're closed today. The power company says they're not sure when we'll be up and running again. The storm knocked out some transformers, among other things."

"Are you okay?" He and his wife lived in a small apartment upstairs in the same building as Caffeine Addiction.

"We're fine. I'll call you when I know more. Go back to sleep, okay?"

"Thanks."

She disconnected and shoved the phone back into her pocket. She wasn't getting any hours today, and the chances were good that the money she would have been paid for tonight's job wasn't happening without power, either.

Derrick was still watching her and waiting for an answer. She glanced down at the table. She could dwell on her problems later.

"It's not my secret to tell." It wasn't an answer, but it was the best she could come up with.

He reached out one big hand and covered hers. "Then whose secret is it? I'd like to help. Maybe we could work together to find Michael and his family."

He had just confirmed that he not only glanced at the letters, he'd read at least one of them. The sinking feeling in her stomach intensified; Holly and her grandma's closely held secret wasn't a secret anymore. The timer she'd set on the stove went off. She got up from the table again to pull the food out of the oven.

"Do you wonder if Michael and his family are sitting in a freezing-cold house right now?" he said. "What if we could help them? I saw some of the other letters. One of those kids asked for a bat, a mitt, and some cleats. I could fulfill every wish in those letters, including paying for a headhunter to find Michael's mom a good job..."

"The median income here is pretty high," she hedged. "Most of those kids will get all that and more from Santa on Christmas morning." She shoveled a couple of pieces of pizza onto a plate, grabbed a fork out of the drawer, and brought it back to the table.

"Then let me help Michael and his family, if we can find them," he coaxed. His voice dropped. "Your grandma can't write anything right now with her hands wrapped up like that," he said.

He *knew*.

She wanted to tell him the whole story so badly, tell him everything that was in her heart about how she'd be willing to help Michael's family with her own money if they needed it, and if she could find them. She'd miss the quarter at UW or have to borrow her tuition, but she would never regret it. She could tell him that her grandma told her she'd never received a Santa letter like that in thirty years. She could only imagine what Derrick's resources could do for a family that needed them so desperately.

She got to her feet and tried to keep her voice casual. "I'd better grab a shower. I'll be back in a few minutes." She reached into her pocket and put her cell phone down on the kitchen table. "It's too dangerous for you to go outside right now to get your charger. You can use my phone to call whomever you'd like. The charger's on the counter."

She got up from the table and went to her room, shutting the door quietly behind her.

DERRICK HEARD MISS Ruth's shuffling steps down the hallway a few minutes later as the shower went on.

"I smell coffee," she called out.

"It's in here," he said.

"I hope you won't mind my casual dress," she told him as she strolled into the kitchen. If he wasn't already awake, her attire made sure of it. She wore neon-green satiny pajamas and a shocking pink chenille robe. She'd tied a red bandana around her hair too. His mama and grandma made some crazy fashion choices at times, but Holly's grandmother took things to an entirely new level.

"Miss Ruth, I do believe you've outdone both my mama and my grandma."

She grinned at him. "It's my job." She grabbed another mug out of the cupboard, flinched a little at holding anything in her hand, and sat down at the table with him. He remembered how much fun it was to try to do things for himself after having a badly broken thumb operated on a couple of years ago. "Is Holly getting ready for work?" she asked.

"No, ma'am. The power is out at the place she works." Derrick poured Holly's grandmother a cup of coffee out of the carafe that still sat on a hot mat on the kitchen table. "Would you like me to get you some sugar?"

"No, thank you."

"How about a piece of pizza? I see there's a piece left, and it just came out of the oven a few minutes ago."

"I can get it," she said.

"No. You relax." He got up from his chair, found a plate, and dished up the food. He put the plate down in front of her.

"Holly's in the shower." He gazed into Miss Ruth's green eyes. "I asked her about the letters. I think she's upset."

"Letters?" Miss Ruth said. Her eyes shifted away from his toward the pile on the table. "What letters?"

"We're not going to do this, are we?"

She took a sip of coffee and stalled for a few seconds. "No. You're right. You do realize, however, that this has been a secret for thirty years, and there will be a lot of disappointed children if it ever gets out…"

"I've heard about that already, and I'm pretty good at keeping a secret." He reached over the table and patted her upper arm. "So, Miss Ruth, there's at least one family in these letters that needs some serious help. I'd like to help them, and you can keep my involvement secret. I have a couple of ideas on how to do this." He stared into her eyes. "I wonder if you'll help me implement them."

She gave him a nod.

Chapter Seven

DERRICK REACHED ACROSS the table to give Miss Ruth's hands a gentle pat. "I'm going to find Michael and his family. I'm also hoping you know enough of these kids to know if someone else might need my help this holiday season too. Let's work together."

"How are we going to explain it to all of these kids?"

"We don't have to explain a thing. Holly may have mentioned to me that most of these families will be taking care of the big gifts themselves."

"She did, did she?" Ruth said. "I'll have to talk with her about spilling my secrets."

"Don't be mad at her. It's not her fault. I fight dirty, Miss Ruth. I wasn't letting up until she told me." She tried to look stern, but he saw her smile. "Why don't we invite the letter writers and their parents to a holiday party here, the local Santa hands out gifts, and I pay for it all?" He leaned back in his chair. "I'll get some idea of how many boys and girls there are and take care of some fun stuff for them. Stuff like games, jump ropes, that kind of thing. I'll figure out how to help Michael's family without their ever knowing who did it, either. How about it?"

Holly's grandmother reached across the table to pat his cheek with a bandaged hand. "I don't know how you're going to pull this off, Derrick, but if you're willing to try, I can help." She got up from the table, walked over to a drawer beneath the counter, and extracted an old-fashioned paper address book. "Here's where we need to start." She flipped the book open so he could see. "Let's talk to Santa Claus first."

HOLLY PUT THE final touches on her hair before she went back to the kitchen. She knew she'd overreacted to Derrick's offer to help, but she knew how much the Santa letters had meant to her grandma over the years. It was a chance for her to give back to Noel, and she looked forward to it each year.

Holly was more touched than she could ever explain to him that Derrick wanted to help people in her community, but she also didn't want him to think the only way anyone cared about him was when he pulled out his wallet.

Maybe she should let everyone else worry about their feelings. She could only be responsible for her own.

She heard her grandma's soft voice from the kitchen, and Derrick's laughter. She peeked around the doorway to see what they were doing. They were bent over the kitchen table with the letters, carefully paper-clipping the envelopes to them while they worked so nothing would get separated. Derrick took notes in her notebook while her grandma read off the items. "So far, we have twenty-five primary letter writers and twelve additional siblings with eighteen more letters to open. Here's another little girl. She says her brother wants a Sharks jersey."

"Did he say which one? I'll bet I can rustle up at least one of those. It might have an autograph on it too." She saw the flash of Derrick's brilliant smile. "Maybe more than one."

"That's nice of you, Derrick," Holly said as she walked into the kitchen. She tried to conceal her amazement that not only was her grandma allowing Derrick to help her read the letters, they were evidently conspiring together as well.

"There you are," he said. He got up from the chair and reached out to hug Holly. "I didn't mean to crowd you out of the action earlier," he said into her ear.

"I'm sorry too."

"You didn't do anything wrong."

"I left. It was rude," she said. "I'm so happy you want to help."

"If you're both done apologizing to each other, we have a lot to do," her grandma said, but she was chuckling as she said it. "Holly, he told me he fights dirty."

Holly let out a sigh. "I collapsed like a house of cards."

Holly's phone rang in Derrick's pocket. He pulled it out and handed it to her.

It was her boss again. "Holly, the Merchants' Association event is postponed too. They just cancelled the mobile espresso cart."

"That's awful. I'm so sorry. I know that's money out of your pocket."

"They'll reschedule." Her boss was quiet for a moment. "Listen. I know this is tough on you financially too. I'm paying you for today. We'll call it a holiday bonus."

Holly clapped one hand over her mouth in surprise. "Thank you. Thank you so much. I'm back at school soon, and I wasn't sure how I was going to make it—"

He interrupted her. "We wish we had more to give, but maybe this will help a bit. Do something you'll enjoy today. Hopefully we'll be ready to go tomorrow morning, and I'll see you then."

"I'll be there. Thank you again."

"You're very welcome, Holly." He disconnected, and she stared at her phone in shock.

"I'm guessing Gil told you he's paying you today," her grandma said as Derrick gave her one more squeeze. Hugging him was like wrapping her arms around a life-sized teddy bear; he was warm, he smelled good, and she felt so protected in his embrace.

"He did," Holly said. "It's really kind of him to do this."

"You deserve it, honey. You work hard for him. Now, let's get busy while you have a little extra time today," her grandma said.

WHILE HOLLY AND her grandma nailed down a local hall on the date Derrick specified, made a deal with the local caterer, and hired the local Santa Claus to make a triumphant appearance, Derrick went into Miss Ruth's family room to call his coach and teammates. He was expecting a monster fine. He would most likely not be playing Sunday afternoon even if he could get back across the pass, which was looking somewhat iffy at this time.

The snow and wind appeared to be slowing down, but he hadn't heard a car pass on the street outside all morning. In other words, the snow was deep and probably meant the roads were impassable. He had no idea how he was getting home, but he'd better come up with something. The team would be practicing hard for Sunday's game.

No matter how big the fine was, it was worth every penny to spend the past several hours with Holly. They'd spent a lot of time dwelling on the letters, but it gave him a chance to see what kind of woman she was. She was thoughtful, kind, caring, and seemed to be as beautiful on the inside as she was to look at. She was exactly what he hoped she would be. He was going to do whatever he had to do to see her at every opportunity. The other women he'd dated in the past would hint around about the school bills she was struggling so hard to pay or ask him outright for a better phone. Not her. She worked for the things she got. He'd seen her reaction when her boss gave her a day off with pay. Despite the fact that she appeared to have little, she was willing to share what she had with him.

There was a surprise coming for her, too: A brand-new smart phone with a contract he was paying for was on its way to her house. It was a damn good thing he called her cell provider before he called half of Bellevue to tell them what was going on with him. She would have paid a fortune for the old-fashioned minutes he used. He'd tried texting with her "dumb" phone, as she called it. It was so frustrating he wanted to let out a string of obscenities and smash the thing on the floor. Holly would be able to text on a state-of-the-art phone. They could stay in touch even with a mountain range between them.

He glanced at the digital clock on her phone. Eleven oh one in the morning; his teammates would be in the weight room, and he needed to man up and call the coach. He punched in the number to the team's front office.

"Seattle Sharks," the receptionist said. "How can I direct your call?"

"Hi, Molly," he said. "It's Derrick Collins. May I talk to Coach Stewart?"

"Of course," she said. "One moment, please."

His coach answered on the third ring. "Collins, where the hell are you?"

"I'm in Noel," Derrick said. "I will get out of here as fast as I can. I know there will be fines."

His normally calm, collected coach was breathing fire.

"Damn right there will be fines, and I'm going to yell at you too. What the fuck? You know we're playing Denver on Sunday. Get your ass back here, son. Would you mind explaining to me exactly why you decided to cross the pass during the season? Did you not watch the weather report? We need you here." The coach pulled in a huge breath. "I should bench you."

"And I would deserve it. I will be back as soon as I can get out of here. I promise."

"Did you just say you deserved to be benched for this one? I must be hearing things. You'd better have a damn good reason why you did this." Maybe it was Derrick's imagination, but the coach seemed to be running out of steam.

"I do. While we're on the phone, Coach, I'm working on a little project for some deserving kids in Noel. I wonder if you'd help me out."

"I'll help you out when you get back here, Collins."

"Got it."

"Keep me updated," the coach said.

"I'll do that." Derrick smiled a little. "Thanks, Coach."

He heard a burst of laughter before the coach hung up. All he had to do now was figure out how he was getting home, and how he was going to see Holly again.

THE STORM FINALLY blew itself out a couple of hours later. Holly could hear the TV on low volume in the living room while Grandma and Derrick tried to figure out what the situation was at the pass. So far, almost a foot of snow had fallen in Noel, and plows were still clearing off the passes back to Seattle. At least the avalanches had stopped.

Holly sat at the kitchen table, handwriting responses to the Santa letters while she added the accounting of girls and boys to Derrick's shopping list, which was getting pretty long and even more expensive.

Derrick walked into the kitchen seconds later and put her phone down in front of her on the table. "I didn't want to forget to give this back," he said.

"Thanks," she said.

"By the way, I paid the unlimited talk and text fee at your cell provider. I didn't want you to have to pay for all the minutes I racked up this morning." He let out a sigh. "Lots and lots of talking. I think I'm exhausted now." He dropped into the chair across from her.

"Derrick, you didn't have to do that," she scolded. "This all is costing you so much money…"

"I have a few dollars in the bank, girl. Don't worry about it."

"But you're already paying for the big party and food and gifts. Didn't you say the coach is mad and he's going to fine you, too? You didn't come over here to spend thousands."

He sat up a bit in his chair and reached out to take her hand. "That's right. I came over here to have dinner with you, and I want to have dinner with you again. How are we going to work this?"

"What do you mean? I don't understand."

"It looks like driving across the pass and I don't quite get along. I found out there's a municipal airport five miles from here. Would you be willing to fly to my place if they brought you back the same night?"

"Derrick, that's…I…it's just wintertime. When the road is cleared off and de-iced, it's not so bad. I promise. That's not it, though," she said. "I can drive to see you if that's what you're worried about. Mostly, though, it's figuring out when this will happen." She let out a sigh. "I work all the time. When I'm not working, I'm at home with Grandma. When she's better, it'll be different, but then I'll be back in school, and I have homework, and"— she couldn't look into his eyes—"I don't know how I can make this work."

He didn't let go of her hand. "So, it's not me. It's the fact that you're trying to do it all at once."

"I'll be out of school in June, and then I have to find a job."

He moved closer to her. "A job, huh?"

"I want to stay in Seattle, but nursing jobs can be tough to find. I—"

He reached up to put gentle fingertips over her lips.

"I'll help you work it all out. I promise I will."

Chapter Eight

TWO DAYS LATER, Holly was alone in Caffeine Addiction at eight AM. Business had picked up since the passes reopened, but she wondered why things weren't jumping as usual. Maybe everyone in Noel had decided they could live without caffeine.

"Yeah, right," she muttered to herself.

She wiped the counter down for the third time in an hour and tried not to stare at the clock. She enjoyed her job, but being busy meant the hours would pass faster. She, Grandma, and Derrick had joined forces to find Michael, and had struck out with every option they had tried. The elementary school principal thought he might be in junior high, but with no siblings' names to go on, they couldn't possibly identify his family. The junior high principal cited confidentiality concerns, but told them there were seven Michaels at his school. All seven had siblings.

Santa Claus told Holly's grandma he'd do his best to ask around town and see what he could come up with. With the Noel Merchants' Association's help, they'd plastered the town with flyers advertising next week's party. If Michael and his family were in town, they couldn't miss it.

Derrick had hired one of the pizza guys to drive Derrick home from Noel in his Escalade when the pass finally opened up the night before last. He'd also paid for a helicopter pilot to fly the pizza guy back to Noel with a bagful of autographed Sharks swag for his trouble.

He'd called Holly when he got home, he'd called her last night, and he said he'd call her when practice was over for the day. It was a good thing she had unlimited minutes on her phone right now. Besides status reports on next week's Santa party, they were asking each other the questions they should have asked on their first date. They talked for hours.

Derrick was quite a storyteller. He made her laugh while he told her anecdotes about growing up with his little brother, Trevon, in a small town in Alabama. Their family wasn't rich, either, and his grandma and parents worked hard to make sure Derrick and his brother had a roof over their heads, food to eat, and clothes on their backs. He told her how much it meant to him that he could make sure the people he loved were taken care of now.

During those hours of conversation, Holly forgot her shyness while she talked and laughed with him. Derrick coaxed her life story out of her, too, as well as asking her what she hoped for in the future. It was hard to believe she felt such a bond with a man after just a week. She fought the nagging fear that real life might never measure up to their sweetly blossoming relationship.

He was the life of the party; she'd rather hide in a corner. She was careful with expressing her feelings. He wore his heart on his sleeve. She scrimped and saved. He'd never have to worry about money again. His encouragement and his interest in her proved to be contagious, though.

"You know that song," he'd said to her last night. "'Started at the bottom, and now we're here'? The only one that can stop you from helping yourself to the things you want in life is you, boo."

"Boo?" she said. She'd heard the nickname before, but she loved hearing it from him.

"My girl. My sweetie. You," he said. She dropped the phone when she hugged herself from sheer happiness.

Derrick also teased her incessantly about their second date, which probably wasn't happening for at least another couple of weeks. He had a game, which her work schedule didn't allow her to even watch. They'd both be at the Santa party, but she would be working for the caterer that night instead of visiting with Derrick.

"I'll get my happy ass over there," Derrick said. "When the party's over, I'll take you out for a soda and hold your hand a little before I go back home." His voice dropped. "I might steal a kiss or two. How's that?"

"Perfect." She sighed.

She was so distracted with daydreaming about Derrick that she didn't notice a woman walking into the coffee shop until she was standing in front of the counter. Holly jumped a little.

"Good morning," Holly said. "What can I get for you?"

The woman appeared to be in her late thirties or early forties, with dark hair and dark eyes. Her expression was wary. A worn scarf was wrapped around her head to keep out the cold. The sleeves on her oversized coat were frayed slightly. She clasped work-worn hands on the counter in front of her. She licked her lips nervously.

"Nothing right now," the woman said. Holly saw her eyes slide to the glass case full of pastries, but she forced herself to look away. "Are you hiring? I'd like to fill out an application, please."

Holly knew they weren't hiring, but there were blank applications under the counter all the time. The woman fidgeted nervously. There were dark circles under her eyes too. She forced her eyes off of the pastries in the case one more time. The hair stood up on the back of Holly's neck as the realization hit her: This woman was hungry, and she hadn't eaten for a while. She needed a job, but first she needed something to eat.

"I don't know what our hiring situation is," Holly said, "but let me get you an application. Why don't you have a seat at the counter while you fill it out?"

"I can go sit at a table or something—"

"That won't be necessary. Really. I'd like the company." Holly reached beneath the counter to grab a blank application and a pen. "Let me get you a glass of water. Do you like coffee?"

She saw the momentary flash of fear and desperation that crossed the woman's face. Her shoulders slumped. She probably didn't have any money in her pocket. Holly could put enough in the till to cover a coffee and a breakfast sandwich, if the woman would accept it.

She wondered how many other applications the woman had filled out in Noel, and if anyone else had noticed the fact things weren't going well for her.

"I...it's good, but I don't need any right now."

"There's a special this morning. Everyone who comes in to fill out an application gets a good breakfast." Holly reached out to briefly touch one of the woman's trembling hands. "It's on the house."

The woman's head bowed. She picked up the pen and the application and glanced at Holly again. "Are you sure?"

"Positive. What would you like?"

Holly made the woman a double-shot latte. She assembled two breakfast sandwiches, wrapping one up to go. She put some cut fruit on the plate too. She wasn't in the business of handing out her boss's food with no charge, but she knew he would have done the same thing. Holly crouched beneath the counter to grab the ten dollar bill out of her wallet. She'd put it in the till when the woman wasn't looking.

The woman was still working on the application when Holly set the plate and coffee cup down in front of her. "Time for breakfast," Holly said.

"Why are you doing this for me?" the woman said.

"You'll pass it on to someone else who needs it when you can," Holly said. She wiped down the countertop again. "Do you know how to work an espresso machine?"

The woman shook her head a little.

"It's not that hard," Holly encouraged.

The woman took a long, appreciative sniff of the coffee and brought the cup to her lips to sip delicately. She wanted to make it last. "I'm a fast learner," the woman said.

Holly gave her a nod and reached across the counter to shake her hand. "I'm Holly, by the way."

"I'm Stephanie," the woman said. "Thank you for the coffee and the breakfast. It's delicious."

Holly did a little more cleaning and stocked the condiments bar while she covertly checked Stephanie out. There was black duct tape holding the sole of one of her snow boots on. She was clean and presentable, but it looked like she really, really needed a job. Stephanie also cut her breakfast sandwich in half, wrapped the other half in a napkin, and slid it into her pocket. No wonder she was hungry; she was sharing the food Holly gave her with someone else, it looked like.

Holly strolled back behind the counter again to glance over the finished application and stick the extra wrapped breakfast sandwich in a bag. She added a couple of pastries for the hell of it. There was enough in the tip jar to cover that amount. She plunked herself down on the bar stool behind Caffeine Addiction's counter.

"Is there anything else I can get for you, Stephanie?"

"No, thank you. Thank you again for the breakfast and the coffee. If you need a resume or something besides what I wrote down, I can get that to you." Stephanie rose from the stool she'd been sitting on, and Holly said, "Wait."

Stephanie turned back to her.

"I-I need to ask you a question," Holly said. "You have people at home who are hungry, too, don't you?"

Stephanie folded her lips and bowed her head again. "I just need a job. If I could find a job, I think we'd be okay. I...I got laid off, I haven't been able to find another job, and I've applied everywhere." She let out a sigh. "I know you didn't ask for this today, but I have to tell someone. My husband left us. My unemployment is running out. I don't know how I'm going to find the money to give my kids a Christmas, let alone how I'm going to pay next month's bills." Her mouth trembled. She looked into Holly's eyes. "I'm so sorry to dump on you."

"How many kids do you have?"

"Three. Michael's fourteen. He's my rock." It was all Holly could do not to punch the air with excitement as Stephanie spoke. "He's had to take care of my younger son and daughter so many times while I interviewed or filled out applications, and he never complains. He's a growing boy. He needs good nourishing food; he's outgrowing his clothes"—tears rose in her eyes, and she silently fought them back—"Ethan's my seven-year-old, and Chloe is my baby. She's four."

"Your contact info is on here, right?" Holly picked up the application to check for an address and phone number.

The fear in Stephanie's face clutched at Holly's guts. "Things aren't great for us right now, but please don't turn me in to Child Protective Services. I don't want to lose my kids. I'll get past this and we'll be fine."

"I wouldn't do that," Holly said. "I want to help." She grabbed the bag of food she'd assembled and walked out from behind the counter. "I know you're doing the best you can. I also know people here who will help." She grabbed the pen still sitting on the counter and scrawled her phone number on the bag of food. "Here's a snack for your family. I will call you when I get home later. Let's work on finding you a great job for starters, okay?" She held out her arms to Stephanie. "Everything is going to be fine. I promise you."

She felt Stephanie's body shaking with sobs as she hugged her.

Chapter Nine

DERRICK SAUNTERED INTO Noel's community center, which had been transformed into a winter wonderland for tonight's party by a group of event planners and a caterer. He glanced around at round tables covered in butcher paper, boxes of crayons at each place setting so the kids could draw while they ate what he'd been assured was excellent food, and centerpieces made of all different sizes of candy canes. A wall-length buffet was under construction. Santa's seat of honor was waiting for him, and so was a photographer who would take souvenir pictures for each child.

Holding the party for the Santa letter-writing children of Noel on a Tuesday turned out to be a stroke of genius. Noel's vendors were booked on party weekends, but were happy to have the business on a weeknight. After the Sharks annihilated Denver on Sunday afternoon, it wasn't hard to persuade most of his teammates to spend a few hours of their day off visiting a cute little town and sharing some holiday cheer. The fact that snow wasn't predicted today—he'd booked every seat on the train going back and forth between Seattle and Noel, so nobody had to drive—didn't hurt, either.

The party didn't start for another hour. His team-mates were wandering around Noel's main street, getting a bite to eat, or doing a little holiday shopping. They'd meet up outside the building and walk in shortly after the party started. Right now, he wanted a few minutes with Holly. Alone.

Four days ago, his phone rang shortly after practice was over for the day. He sat down on the bench in front of his locker and hit "talk" to hear Holly's tear-filled voice.

"We found Michael," was all she said.

Michael and his family were due here tonight as well. He couldn't wait to meet them. They'd never know he'd worked behind the scenes with an employment agency to make sure Stephanie found a job. They now had more than enough food, the bills were paid, and it would be the happiest of holidays for them. There was no better feeling in life than knowing he'd done what he could to help a family when they needed it most.

He had an additional surprise for Michael, which would happen later. He headed toward the community center's kitchen. He couldn't wait another minute to see Holly again.

HOLLY TIED AN apron on over the white shirt and black pants she wore to serve at catering jobs, and picked up a pastry bag of chocolate mousse filling. The caterer was racing around the kitchen putting the last-minute touches on her holiday menu. Holly was helping out by piping the mousse into chocolate cookie cups. She was trying to concentrate, but all she could think of at the moment was Derrick. He was due to be there soon with his teammates, who would sign autographs, pose for photos, and help Santa hand out the swag bags. The mousse looked good, but she couldn't have eaten a bite if her life depended on it right now. Her stomach was full of butterflies, her heart raced, and her palms were sweaty.

She was either having a panic attack, or she was excited about seeing Derrick again.

She'd almost finished piping one tray of the chocolate mousse tarts when two strong arms slid around her waist and she heard a deep voice in her ear.

"There's my girl," he said.

She dropped the pastry bag on the worktable in front of her, turned in his arms, and wrapped her arms around his neck. "It's great to see you," she said into his ear.

He pulled back from her a little, glanced around the kitchen, and said, "We're finally alone."

"Only until the caterer comes back."

He moved closer, and her heart pounded harder. He cupped her face in his palm. "Then I have time to do this."

Her eyelids slid closed as his mouth met hers. For a big, tough man, Derrick's kisses were tender and sweet, and his touch was gentle. He slipped his tongue into her mouth when her lips parted. He pulled her closer as he explored and savored her. She forgot all about the chocolate mousse, all about the fact she was supposed to be working, all about anything else but the way he tasted and how it felt to be in his arms.

Someone cleared her throat behind them.

"Oh!", Holly said and moved away from Derrick slightly.

The caterer was standing feet from them and grinning from ear to ear.

"If you'll hand me that tray, Holly, they're going onto the display," she said.

"I'm so sorry," Holly told her. "We got a little, uh, carried away."

"I'm not sorry," Derrick muttered, and the caterer laughed.

"I'll bet you're not," she teased. She picked up another tray full of appetizers and went out the swinging door again.

Holly could feel her face getting hot with embarrassment, but she smiled up at him. "She didn't look too mad, did she?"

He traced her nose with a gentle finger. "Naw." He kissed the middle of her forehead before reluctantly releasing her. "There's more where that came from, you know."

She shivered a little. "I hope so."

His booming laugh bounced around the kitchen. "Hopefully I didn't get you fired. Is there anything I can do to help?"

FORTY-FIVE MINUTES LATER, Santa had taken his place, swag bags were organized and ready to go, Derrick and his teammates were in another room waiting for their cue, and children in their holiday best and their parents began to stream through the front doors of the community center. Holly was passing appetizers and guiding the younger children to the extra-special food made just for them, like the macaroni-and-cheese bar with assorted toppings, sliders, and chicken nuggets with sauces.

She spotted Stephanie and her children when they walked through the door. Stephanie had on a new coat, snow boots, and a radiant smile. Her children were dressed in brand-new clothes and shoes as well. Michael was a dark-haired, athletic-looking young man with a shy smile; he was taller than his mother and guided his younger brother and sister to the buffet to fill their plates.

Stephanie almost ran to Holly.

"You won't believe what happened, Holly. I have a new job. I start at a mortgage lender in Wenatchee on Monday morning. It's a really good salary with benefits, and they cover day care. Plus, the overnight shipping guy stopped at our house yesterday and dropped off presents for the kids, several gift cards for me so I could get everyone new clothes and shoes and…oh, God." Stephanie pressed her hands over her eyes as tears ran down her face. "I never dreamed anything like this would happen to me. There was a tree with all the trimmings, a huge Christmas dinner, and I'm still going through it all."

Holly reached out to hug her. "You deserve it."

"I know you were behind this. I can never thank you enough."

"It wasn't me, but you are so sweet. I am so happy for all of you."

Holly heard Santa Claus's voice on the PA system. "Ladies and gentlemen, we have quite a surprise tonight. Please welcome our special guests, the Seattle Sharks!"

Derrick and his teammates walked into the room, and pandemonium followed. The littlest children were swept up in their parents' arms as the players signed autographs, posed for photos, or sat down at the tables for a bite to eat and a chat with their excited fans.

Tom Reed, the Sharks' QB, made his way over to where Michael stood and stuck out his hand. "Hi, I'm Tom."

Michael's mouth dropped open.

"I understand that you play QB, and you weren't able to turn out for football last season. I also heard you're pretty good."

"My mom needed help with my younger brother and sister," Michael said.

In other words, Holly thought, there probably wasn't enough money for sports fees and football shoes.

"I give a football camp every year." Tom reached into his jacket and pulled a long envelope out of the breast pocket. "I'd like you to be there as my guest. Your tuition is paid, and I have a place for you to stay so your mom won't have to drive you back and forth."

Holly took Stephanie's trembling hand. Her boss was going to kill her for not passing out the appetizers, but she glanced over at the platter in her other hand to find it empty. People were walking by and helping themselves.

Four of Derrick's teammates advanced on Michael and Tom. Sharks fans knew them as the best secondary in the league. She knew them as the four guys who spent most of training camp alternately teasing her and pranking their teammates.

"We heard he's trying to get you to play QB," Terrell said.

"Bad idea," Jasha chimed in.

"Cornerbacks and safeties are the real men of any football team," Conroy told Michael.

"I got my own football camp this summer, and you're coming," Antoine said. He fist-bumped the overwhelmed teenager. "We'll show you how things are."

The five men walked away from Holly and Stephanie, still bickering about how many football camps Michael was going to over the summer and what position he'd end up playing in the league.

"I need to get another tray of appetizers. I'll be back," Holly said.

She arrived in the kitchen to discover the caterer had deputized some of the players to take some appetizers around too. "The kids will get a kick out of it," she explained to them. "Hey, Holly, Derrick's looking for you. He's outside. So take a break." She winked at Holly.

Holly walked out of the double doors of the community center. Derrick was sitting on a bench about ten feet away, holding a bouquet of candy canes tied with a red ribbon.

"Hello there," he said. "Would you like to join me for a few minutes?"

She sat down next to him on the bench, and he pulled her into his warmth. He handed her the candy canes. She had to laugh.

"I love these. Thank you so much."

"That's not all I've got for you tonight," he said. His deep voice made her shiver, and it had nothing to do with the cold. "I want to take you out for a nice dinner and maybe some dancing next week. Let's see if we can put it together."

"Between your schedule and my schedule?"

"Where there's a will, there's a way."

She leaned back against him. "I'll look forward to it." She let out a breath. "Derrick, Stephanie is so happy right now, and Michael is just over the moon."

"My teammates argued the whole way over here about whose football camp he was going to, and who was going to work with him a little during the offseason." She felt the rumble of his laughter. "If that kid has any talent at all, he's going to end up at a very good school."

She laced her fingers through his and closed her eyes.

"Are you feeling shy again?" he said.

"No. I'm just happy."

"There's one more thing. I couldn't wait for Christmas Day. I have a gift for you."

"You didn't have to buy me anything. You put on this huge party, you helped Stephanie's family, you bought me that hugely expensive phone…Derrick, what am I going to get you for Christmas?"

He laid his fingertips over her mouth. "You don't have to buy me a thing."

"It's not fair."

"Okay, then. You win. Bake me some cookies or something. I would love that more than anything."

"What kind?"

"The same kind everyone else wants: chocolate chip."

She couldn't help but laugh. "Got it," she said.

He was fumbling in his coat pocket, and he pulled out a palm-sized Tiffany's box.

"Here's the thing. I saw this and I thought it was perfect for you. I hope you love it as well." He put the box into her hand, and waited expectantly.

She pulled open the ribbon, took off the top of the box, and pulled out the little suede pouch inside. He opened the drawstring top and drew out a small platinum heart, studded with diamonds, on a chain.

"It's gorgeous. It's so extravagant though! I...cookies aren't enough. Isn't there anything else you'd like for Christmas?"

"You already gave me the greatest gift," he said. "Your friendship. Someday, you'll give me your heart too." He fastened the necklace around her neck. She reached up to rest her forehead against his. She rubbed her nose against his too.

"I think I already have," she whispered.

"It's all I'll ever want," he said.

Epilogue

Six months later.

THIS COULD BE the shortest official engagement on record.

Holly Reynolds graduated from the University of Washington two hours ago. Her brand-new fiancé, Derrick, got down on one knee in front of Drumheller Fountain moments after she claimed her hard-won diploma and asked her to marry him. He slid a large, cushion-cut diamond ring surrounded by a halo of smaller diamonds set in platinum onto the third finger of her left hand.

It was a good thing she'd said yes. Two weeks ago, they'd started planning a top-secret wedding. Derrick was still the more outgoing and gregarious one; he would have loved a huge party full of hundreds of people to celebrate their wedding. Holly longed for just a few family and friends as guests on their big day.

"I want to marry you," Derrick had said. "The rest is just details."

"But what about the big party?" she said. "I don't want you to miss it."

"We'll have the people that love us most at our wedding. That's what I want."

The family and friends—and a few of Derrick's teammates—who would be celebrating Holly's graduation with them at downtown Seattle's AQUA this afternoon were in for quite a surprise. Three days ago, Derrick and Holly made a quick and quiet visit to Seattle's City Hall to obtain a marriage license. All other details were being handled by an incredibly competent wedding coordinator, who was currently helping Holly button the back of her wedding dress in a hotel suite a short distance from the restaurant. Holly put on the birdcage veil she'd bought to go with the white, knee-length, three-quarter-sleeved lace sheath while the coordinator used a crochet hook to secure the stubborn satin-covered buttons.

Holly stepped into the cobalt-blue satin high heels she couldn't resist buying. She wore her grandma's pearls: something borrowed. Her wedding dress was something new. She pulled a handkerchief her mom had embroidered with her initials when Holly was a little girl out of her bag.

"I think I'm ready," Holly said. She'd heard before that all brides were nervous. She had told herself that the butterflies in her stomach, her sweaty palms, and her trembling hands were normal. Despite being a bit scared, she couldn't wait to marry Derrick.

The coordinator reached into a floral box and handed her a bouquet of white rosebuds, stephanotis, crystals, and ivy, tied with a wide white double-faced satin bow. "I'll go downstairs and call your phones when everyone's there," she said. "Everything is ready and waiting for you and Derrick." She dug into her pocket and produced a sixpence. "One more thing. A lucky penny for your shoe."

"Thank you so much," Holly said. She reached out to carefully hug the coordinator. "I could never have done this without your help."

"Congratulations, and here's to a lifetime of happiness."

The coordinator left the room, talking into her headset.

Seconds later, Holly heard a tap on the suite's front door, and Derrick's deep voice. "Baby, it's me."

"I'll be right there," Holly said. She pulled Derrick's wedding band out of the box and slid it onto her thumb. She grabbed up her bouquet. It was showtime.

She tugged the door open so he could walk inside, and her breath caught. He looked so handsome in his dark suit and cobalt blue silk tie, with his the dreadlocks pulled back from his face. In the meantime, he was staring at her. She was shocked to see tears swimming in his eyes. His face worked with emotion as he reached out for her hand and brought it to his lips.

"You are so beautiful," he whispered. "I want to remember this moment forever."

She reached up to stroke his cheek. "You're gorgeous too."

He wrapped his arms around her, and she laid her head on his massive shoulder. There was nowhere in the world safer for her than in the circle of Derrick's embrace.

"Let's cut out of the reception early," he said. "We have things to do."

"I'm guessing my grandma would be shocked and horrified at your plans, wouldn't she?"

"So would my mama and my grandma." His voice dropped. "Let me give you a hint or two." His arms tightened around her. "We're coming back here, I'm peeling that dress right off of you, and I'm going to spend as long as it takes to show you and tell you how crazy I am about you." He rested his cheek against the top of her head. "I might not let you put clothes on again."

"Really?" She tipped her head back, looked into his eyes, and said teasingly, "I'm going to marry the hell out of you first."

Their sweet, tender moment was temporarily over. He burst out laughing. "Is that so? We'd better go find the preacher, then." He leaned his forehead against hers. "I love you, boo."

"I love you too. So much," she said.

His cell phone chirped with an incoming text. He grabbed it out of his jacket pocket and took a look at the screen. "They're ready for us." He offered her his arm, and she slipped her hand through it as he held the door open for her.

Their ride in the elevator was almost silent. The doors swooshed open on the correct floor, and people waiting to go upstairs burst into applause when Derrick and Holly stepped out.

"Congratulations," someone called out.

"Aren't you Derrick Collins of the Sharks?" another person said.

"Yes, I am," he said. Holly waved at the cluster of people with her bouquet.

Derrick led her half a block down the street to the luxurious private room their guests waited in. The normally energetic, assertive Derrick was definitely nervous. His palms were sweaty, and he kept licking his lower lip. It was adorable.

He stopped in front of the double doors to the restaurant, took a deep breath, and said, "Ready?"

"Oh yes."

Most of their guests lingered at the floor-to-ceiling windows looking out over Elliott Bay and a seemingly endless blue sky. The water sparkled like diamonds in the June sunshine. Mount Rainier was out today too. The door clicked shut behind them, several of the guests turned to see who'd arrived, and Derrick's voice boomed over the stunned silence.

"Surprise!"

It took thirty seconds or so, but their friends and family clapped and called out questions as they clustered around Holly and Derrick.

"Are you…are you wearing a wedding dress?" her grandma said. "How did I not know about this?"

"You're getting married?" Derrick's mother called out. "Right now?"

"I'm guessing this isn't really a graduation party," Drew McCoy called out. Drew's wife, Cameron, was applauding.

Holly's mom burst into tears. "I'm just so happy," she said.

Holly's roommates clustered around her. "You look gorgeous!"

Derrick had invited most of his teammates, but he didn't want to spoil the surprise, so many sent their best wishes instead of coming back from their various offseason pursuits for a "graduation party." He glanced over at the guys who'd managed to show up. They looked stunned at this development.

One of the defensive line rookies called out, "Wait until the guys find out you got your ass married and they missed it."

"It was nice of me to invite you, wasn't it?" Derrick teased. He glanced over at his mama. "Yes, Mama, we're getting married right now."

The coordinator sped around the room, getting people settled into their seats. The minister took his place at the top of an improvised aisle. Holly reached out to take her roommates' hands.

"Would you be my maids of honor?" she said.

The ever-practical Courtney said, "Of course we will. We both can't sign the license, though."

"We'll flip for it," Courtney's sister, Whitney, said. "Come on."

Holly reached out for her dad's hand.

"How about I walk my favorite girl up the aisle?" her dad said.

"I would love that, Dad. I'm so glad you and Mom are here."

"Nothing could keep us away," he said. He squeezed her hand as he slipped it through her arm. "Best surprise ever, as you kids would say."

Derrick was glancing around, and Holly could almost read his mind: He needed to choose a best man on the spot from the friends and family present.

"Baby, it's whoever you'd like," she whispered to him.

"Yeah. I'll do that," he said. He scanned the room with an anxious look on his face, and turned back to her. "I was really hoping he'd be here."

"I don't understand. Did you invite someone else?" she said.

Seconds later, they heard the latch on the room's door behind them click open, and a voice as deep as Derrick's said, "I didn't miss it all, did I?"

"Trevon," Derrick said. He whirled, throwing his arms around a younger man with closely cropped hair who wore a military dress uniform. "You're here, man."

"I told you I'd make it," his brother said. The two men hugged, slapped each other on the back, and wiped away a few tears.

Trevon held out his hand for Holly's. "You must be my new sister," he said. He brought the back of her hand to his lips and kissed it. "Welcome to the family."

Holly gave him a trembling smile in response. Trevon reached out for his mama and his grandma, who'd hurried across the room to throw their arms around him too.

A few minutes later, Derrick and Trevon took their places next to the minister. Holly slid her hand through her dad's arm again. The DJ cued up John Legend's "All of Me," and Holly was thankful she was wearing waterproof mascara. She knew why Derrick had asked for this song. They both had faults, but she loved him more than anyone else because he had the courage to show his weaknesses to her, accepting and loving her for who she was too.

Holly's parents had moved to Arizona four years ago because her mom's health couldn't take Seattle's damp winters anymore. Retirement definitely agreed with them. Even if they didn't see each other every day anymore, she'd never doubted her parents' love for her. Her dad patted her hand and said, "I look forward to getting to know Derrick."

"I know he wants to spend some time with you, too, Dad. As well as with Mom and Marcus." Holly's older brother, Marcus, lived in Utah with his wife, who was expecting their first child.

"We're so proud of you and we love you very much," her dad said. He stopped at the top of the aisle only feet from Derrick. "Be happy, honey."

"I love you too. Thank you for everything you've done for me," she said.

Her dad kissed her cheek and reached out for Derrick's hand. He was enveloped in a huge bear hug. "Mr. Reynolds," Derrick said.

"Call me 'Dad,'" Holly's father said. Poor Derrick; he needed another handkerchief. Finally, it was the two of them in front of the minister.

"I'd like to welcome everyone to Derrick and Holly's wedding. Who gives this woman to be married to this man?" the minister asked.

"Her mother and I," her dad said. He sat down next to Holly's mother, who was already dabbing at her eyes with a tissue.

Derrick took Holly's hands in both of his. They made promises with trembling voices and slipped a ring onto each other's finger. Finally, Derrick pulled her into his arms for their first kiss as husband and wife. She heard laughter and applause as he kissed her a second time, and then a third. She wrapped her arms around his neck and laid her cheek against his as he spoke up.

"I've been waiting a long time to kiss my wife."

DERRICK WATCHED HOLLY circulate among their thirty-five guests. She was glowing with happiness as she accepted congratulations and held out her hand so their friends and family members could see her rings. They'd danced together, had dinner, cut the cake, and kissed, when yet another guest tapped a glass with a piece of silverware. Shelby Anderson had caught Holly's bouquet. Derrick didn't miss the look of triumph in Shelby's boyfriend Chuck's eyes. Unless he was really wrong, Chuck was about to propose.

Wait until Shelby's big brother, Zach, found out.

Derrick was ready to start their honeymoon, but a few of his teammates were having a fairly interesting convo in one corner as they watched the women in their lives talking and laughing together.

"And another one bites the dust, Collins," Zach Anderson teased. "There aren't many single Sharks around these days. Caleb's dating my kid sister, and Drew McCoy even tied the knot."

"Best decision I ever made," McCoy interrupted. He glanced across the room at his wife, Kendall.

Seth Taylor took a sip of beer in response.

"Taylor," Zach said, "I think your number's up, man. Accept it gracefully."

"Nope. Not getting married," Seth said.

"Are you sure about that?" Derrick shot back. "Care to make it interesting?" He jammed his hand in his suit pocket and pulled out a money clip.

The normally shy and reserved Caleb pulled bills out of his pocket and slapped them down on the table. "Get out your cash, men. Five hundred says that he's engaged before the end of next season."

"Oh, you're on," Seth told them. "Who's holding the cash?"

"I'll do it," Zach said as he dropped his five hundred dollars on the pile.

Derrick added his cash. Drew McCoy laughed at them, but dug into his pocket as well.

"Taking your money will be sweet," Seth said.

"We won't lose," Derrick said. "We don't ever lose. With that, I gotta go." He didn't want to wait one more minute to spend the rest of his life holding Holly.

Keep cheering on the
Seattle Sharks in Julie Brannagh's
next exciting book,

CHASING JILLIAN

Jillian Miller likes her job working in the front office for the Seattle Sharks, but lately, being surrounded by a constant parade of perfection only seems to make her own imperfections all the more obvious. She needs a change, which takes her into foreign territory: the Sharks' workout facility after hours. The last thing she expects is a hot, grumbly god among men to be there as witness.

Star linebacker Seth Taylor has had a bad day—in fact, he's had a series of them recently. When he hits the Sharks' gym to work out his frustration, he's startled to find someone there—and even more surprised that it's Jillian, the team owner's administrative assistant. When he learns of Jillian's mission to revamp her lifestyle, he finds himself volunteering to help. Something about Jillian's beautiful smile and quick wit makes him want to stick around. She may not be like the swimsuit models he usually has on his arm, but the more time Seth spends with Jillian, the harder he falls.

As Jillian learns that the new her is about so much more than what she sees in the mirror, can she discover that happiness and love are oh-so-much better than perfect?

Coming Spring 2015

An Excerpt from

BLITZING EMILY

Love and Football, Book One

Available Now from Avon Impulse!

Emily Hamilton doesn't trust men. She's much more comfortable playing the romantic lead on stage in front of a packed house than in her own life. So, when NFL star and irresistible ladies' man Brandon McKenna acts as her personal white knight, she has no illusions he'll stick around. However, a misunderstanding with the press throws them together in a fake engagement that yields unexpected (and breathtaking) benefits.

Every time Brandon calls her "sugar," Emily almost believes Brandon's playing for keeps, not just to score. Can she let down her defenses and get her own Happily Ever After?

EMILY HAD BARELY enough time to hang up the cordless and flip on the TV before Brandon wandered down the stairs.

"Hey," he said, and he threw himself down on the couch next to her.

His blond curls were tangled, his eyes sleepy, and she saw a pillowcase crease on his cheek. He looked completely innocent until she saw the wicked twinkle in his eyes. Even in dirty workout clothes, he was breathtaking. She wondered if it was possible to ovulate on demand.

"I'm guessing you took a nap," she said.

"I was supposed to be watching you." He tried to look penitent. It wasn't working.

"Glad to know you're making yourself comfortable," she teased.

He stretched his arm around the back of the couch.

"Everything in your room smells like flowers, and your bed's great." He pulled up the edge of his T-shirt and sniffed it. Emily almost drooled at a glimpse of his rock-hard abdomen. Evidently, it was possible to have more than a six pack. "The guys will love my new perfume. Maybe they'll want some makeup tips," he muttered, and grabbed for the remote Emily left on the coffee table.

He clicked through the channels at a rapid pace.

"Excuse me. I had that." She lunged for it. No such luck. Emily ended up sprawled across his lap.

"The operative word here, sugar, is 'had.'" He held it up in the air out of her reach while he continued to click. He'd wear a hole in his thumb if he kept this up. "No NFL Network." She tried to sit up again, which wasn't working well. Of course, he was chuckling at her struggles. "Oh, I get it. You're heading for second base."

"Hardly." Emily reached over and tried to push off on the other arm of the couch. One beefy arm wrapped around her. "I'm not trying to do anything. Oh, whatever."

"You know, if you want a kiss, all you have to do is ask."

She couldn't imagine how he managed to look so innocent while smirking.

"I haven't had a woman throw herself in my lap for a while now. This could be interesting," he said.

Emily's eyebrows shot to her hairline. "I did not throw myself in your lap."

"Could've fooled me. Which one of us is—"

"Let go of me." She was still trying to grab the remote, without success.

"You'll fall," he warned.

"What's your point?"

"Here." He stuck the remote down the side of the couch cushion so Emily couldn't grab it. He grasped her upper arms, righted her with no effort at all, and looked into her eyes. "All better. Shouldn't you be resting, anyway?"

Emily tried to take a breath. Their bodies were frozen. He held her, and she gazed into his face. His dimple appeared, vanished, appeared again. She licked her lips with the microscopic amount of moisture left in her mouth. He was fighting a smile, but even more, he dipped his head toward her. He was going to kiss her.

"Yes," she said.

Her voice sounded weak, but it was all she could do to push it out of lungs that had no air at all. He continued to watch her, and he gradually moved closer. Their mouths were inches apart. Emily couldn't stop looking at his lips. After a few moments that seemed like an eternity, he released her and dug the remote from the couch cushion. She felt a stab of disappointment. He had changed his mind.

"Turns out you have the NFL Network, so I think I can handle another twenty-four hours here," he announced as he stopped on a channel she'd never seen before.

"You might not be here another twenty-four minutes. Don't you have a TV at home?" She wrapped her arms around her midsection. She wished she could come up with something more witty and cutting to say. She was so sure he would kiss her, and then he hadn't.

An Excerpt from

RUSHING AMY

Love and Football, Book Two

Available Now from Avon Impulse!

*For Amy Hamilton, only three F's matter: Family,
Football, and Flowers. It might be nice to find someone
to share Forever with too, but right now she's working
double overtime while she gets her flower shop off
the ground. The last thing she needs or wants is a
distraction…or help, for that matter. Especially in the
form of gorgeous and aggravatingly arrogant ex-NFL
star Matt Stephens.*

*Matt lives by a playbook—his playbook. He never thought
his toughest opponent would come in the form of a
stunning florist with a stubborn streak to match his own.
Since meeting her in the bar after her sister's wedding, he's
known there's something between them. When she refuses,
again and again, to go out with him, Matt will do anything
to win her heart…But will Amy, who has everything to
lose, let the clock run out on the one-yard line?*

THE WEDDING WAS over, and Amy Hamilton stood among the wreckage.

Every flat surface in the Woodmark Hotel's grand ballroom was strewn with dirty plates, empty glasses, crumpled napkins, spent champagne bottles—the outward indication that a large group of people had one hell of a party. A few hours ago, Amy's older sister, Emily, had married Brandon McKenna, the man of her dreams.

Three hundred guests toasted the bride and groom repeatedly. Happy tears flowed as freely as the champagne. The dinner was delicious, the cake, even better. The newlyweds and their guests danced to a live band till after midnight. The hotel ballroom was transformed into a candlelit fairyland for her sister's flawless evening, but now all that was left was the mess. The perfectly arranged profusion of flowers was drooping. So was she.

Amy arranged flowers for weddings almost every weekend. Doing the flowers for Emily's wedding, though, was an extra-special thrill. She'd seen it all over the past few years, first as an apprentice to another florist, and then after opening her own shop a little over a year ago. It meant long hours and hard work, but she was determined her business would succeed.

Amy took a last look at the twinkling lights of the boats crossing Lake Washington through the floor-to-ceiling windows along the west wall. She couldn't help but notice she stood alone in a room that had been packed with people only an hour or so ago. She'd been alone for a long time now, and she didn't like the feeling at all. She picked up the black silk chiffon wrap draped over yet another chair, and the now-wilting bridal bouquet Emily had tossed to her. Obviously, she'd stalled long enough. She wondered if the kitchen staff would mind whipping up a vat of chocolate mousse to drown her sorrows in.

Heavy footsteps sounded behind Amy on the ballroom floor, and she turned toward them. The man she'd watched on a hundred *NFL Today* pregame broadcasts strolled toward her. Any woman with a pulse knew who he was, let alone any woman hopelessly addicted to Pro Sports Network.

Matt Stephens was tall. His body, sculpted by years of workouts, was showcased in a perfectly tailored navy suit, but that didn't tell the whole story. The wavy, slightly mussed blue-black hair, the square jaw, the olive skin that seemed to glow, and the flawless, white smile were exactly what Amy saw on her television screen each week during football season. Television didn't do him justice. After all, on her TV screen he didn't prowl. He locked eyes with her as he crossed the ballroom.

She glanced around to confirm she was still alone in the ballroom, and the beeline he was making was actually toward her. She couldn't imagine what he wanted.

She knew a lot about him. Matt was a former NFL star, and a good friend of her new brother-in-law. When Matt got tired of playing with the Dallas Cowboys (three Super Bowl rings and six visits to the Pro Bowl later), he'd played in Seattle for the last two years of his career, afterward embarking on the wide world of game analysis and product endorsements. Guys wanted to be him, and women just plain wanted him.

Well, women who were still on the playing field wanted him. She was putting herself on injured reserve. After all, *once burned, twice shy,* and every other cliché she'd ever heard that reminded her of salt being poured on the open wound that was her heart.

Mostly, guys who looked like Matt weren't looking for someone like her: A woman more interested in being independent than being some guy's arm candy.

Matt stopped a few feet away from Amy. The deep dimples on either side of his lips flashed as his mouth moved into an irresistible grin.

"Hello, there."

"You're late." The words flew out of her mouth before she realized she'd said it aloud.

An Excerpt from

CATCHING CAMERON

Love and Football, Book Three

Available Now from Avon Impulse!

*Star sports reporter Cameron Ondine has one
firm rule: she does not date football players. Ever. She
tangled with one years ago, and it did not end well. Been
there, done that. But when Cameron comes face to face
with the very man who shattered her heart—on camera,
no less—her world is upended for a second time by
recklessly handsome Seattle Shark Zach Anderson.*

*Zach has never been able to forget the gorgeous blonde
who stole his breath away when he was still just a rookie.
They've managed to give each other a wide berth for
years, but when he and Cameron are suddenly forced to
live in close quarters for a TV stunt, he knows he
has to face his past once and for all. Because the more
time they spend together, the less he's focused on the
action on the field and the more concerned
he is with catching Cameron.*

ZACH ANDERSON WAS in New York City again, and he wasn't happy about it. He wasn't big on crowds as a rule, except for the ones that spent Sunday afternoons six months a year cheering for him as he flattened yet another offensive lineman on his way to the guy's quarterback. He also wasn't big on having four people fussing over his hair, spraying him down with whatever it was that simulated sweat, and trying to convince him that nobody would ever know he was wearing bronzer in the resulting photos.

Then again, he was making eight figures for a national Under Armour campaign for two days' work; maybe he shouldn't bitch. The worst injury he might sustain here would be some kind of muscle pull from running away from the multiple women hanging out at the photo shoot who had already made it clear they'd be interested in spending more time with him.

He was all dolled up in UA's latest. Of course, he typically didn't wear workout clothes that were tailored or ironed before he pulled them on. The photo shoot was now in its second hour, and he was wondering how many damn pictures of him they actually needed. There were worse things than being a pro football player who looked like the cover model on a workout magazine, was followed around by large numbers of hot young women, and got paid for it all.

"Gorgeous," the photographer shouted to him. "Okay, Zach. I need pensive. Thoughtful. Sensitive."

Zach shook his head briefly. "You're shitting me."

Zach's agent, Jason, shoved himself off the back wall of the room and moved into Zach's line of vision. Jason had been with him since Zach signed his first NFL contract. He was also a few years older than Zach, which came in handy. He took the long view in his professional and personal life, and encouraged Zach to do so as well.

"Come on, man. Think about the poor polar bears starving to death because they can't find enough food at the North Pole. How about the NFL going to eighteen games in the regular season? If that's not enough, *Sports Illustrated*'s discontinuing the swimsuit issue could make a grown man cry." Even the photographer snorted at that last one. "You can do it."

Eighteen games a season would piss Zach off more than anything else, but he gazed in the direction the photographer's assistant indicated, thought about how long it would take him to get across town to his appointment when this was over, and listened to the camera's rapid clicking once more.

"Are you sure you want to keep playing football?" the photographer called out. "The camera loves you."

"Thanks," Zach muttered. Shit. How embarrassing. If any of his four younger sisters were here right now, they'd be in hysterics.

CAMERON SMILED INTO the camera for the last time today. "Thanks for watching. I'm Cameron Ondine, and I'll see you next week on *NFL Confidential*." She waited until the floor director gave her the signal the camera was off, and stood up to stretch. Today's guest had been a twenty-five year old quarterback who'd just signed a five-year contract with Baltimore's team for seventy-five million dollars. Fifty million of it was guaranteed. His agent hovered off-camera, but not close enough to prevent the guy in question from asking Cameron to accompany him to his hotel suite to "hook up."

Cameron wished she were surprised about such invitations, but they happened with depressing frequency. The network wanted her to play up what she had to offer: fresh-faced, wholesome beauty, a body she worked ninety minutes a day to maintain, and a personality that proved she wasn't just another dumb blonde. She loved her job, but she didn't love the fact some of these guys thought sleeping with her was part of the deal her employers offered when she interviewed them.

An Excerpt from

COVERING KENDALL

Love and Football, Book Four

Available Now from Avon Impulse!

*Kendall Tracy, general manager of the San Francisco
Miners, is not one for rash decisions or one-night stands.
But when she finds herself alone in a hotel room with a
heart-stoppingly gorgeous man who looks oddly familiar,
Kendall throws her own rules out the window...and they
blow right back into her face.*

*Drew McCoy should look familiar; he's a star player for
her team's archrival the Seattle Sharks. Which would
basically make Drew and Kendall the Romeo and Juliet
of professional football...well, without all the dying. Not
that it's an issue. They agree to pretend their encounter
never happened. Nothing good can come from it
anyway, right?*

*Drew's not so sure. Kendall may be all wrong, but
he can't stop thinking about her and he finds that some*

risks are worth taking. Because the stakes are always
highest when you're playing for keeps.

"YOU'RE DREW MCCOY," she cried out.

She scooted to the edge of the bed, clutching the sheet around her torso as she went. It was a little late now for modesty. Retaining some shred of dignity might be a good thing.

She'd watched Drew's game film with the coaching staff. She'd seen his commercials for hair products and sports drink and soup a hundred times before. His contract with the Sharks was done as of the end of football season, and the Miners wanted him to play for them. Drew was San Francisco's number one target in next season's free agency. She'd planned on asking the team's owner to write a big check to Drew and his agent next March. If all that wasn't enough, Drew was eight years younger than she was.

What the hell was wrong with her? It must have been the knit hat covering his famous hair, or finding him in a nonjock hangout like a bookstore. Maybe it was the temporary insanity brought on by an overwhelming surge of hormones.

"Is there a problem?" he said.

"I can't have anything to do with you. I have to go."

He shook his head in adorable confusion. She couldn't think of anything she wanted more right now than to run her fingers through his gorgeous hair.

"This is your hotel room. Where do you think you're going?"

She yanked as much of the sheet off the bed as possible, attempting to wrap it around herself and stand up at the same time. He was simultaneously grabbing at the comforter to shield himself. It didn't work.

She twisted her foot into the bedding while she hurled herself away from him and ended up on the carpet seconds later in a tangle of sheet and limbs, still naked. Her butt hit the floor so hard she almost expected to bounce.

The number-one reason why Kendall didn't engage in one-night stands as a habit hauled himself up on all fours in the middle of the bed. Out of all the guys in the world available for a short-term fling, of all the times in her life she thought that might be an acceptable option, of *course* she'd pick the man who could get her fired or sued.

He grabbed the robe he'd slung over the foot of the bed, scrambled off the mattress, and jammed his arms into it as he advanced on her.

"Are you okay? You went down pretty hard." His eyes skimmed over her. "That's going to leave a mark."

He crouched next to her as he reached out to help her up. She resisted the impulse to stare at golden skin, an eight pack, and a sizable erection. She'd heard Drew didn't lack for dates. He had other things to offer besides the balance in his bank accounts.

"I'm okay," she told him.

She felt a little shaky. She'd probably have a nice bruise later. She was going down all right, and it had nothing to do with sex. It had everything to do with the fact that if anyone from the Miners organization saw him emerging from her room in the next seventy-two hours, she was in the kind of trouble with her employer there was no recovering from. The interim general manager of a NFL team did not sleep with anyone from the opposing team, especially arch-rivals that hated each other with the heat of a thousand suns. Especially a star player her own organization was more than a little interested in acquiring. *Especially* before a game that would mean the inside track to the playoffs for both teams.

Drew and Kendall would be the Romeo and Juliet of the NFL. Well, without all the dying. Death by 24/7 sports media embarrassment didn't count.

He reached out, grabbed her beneath her armpits, and hoisted her off the floor like she weighed nothing.

"I've got you. Let's see if you can stand up," he said. His warm, gentle hands moved over her, looking for injuries. "Why don't you lean on me for a second here?"

She tried rewrapping the sheet around her so she could walk away from him while preserving her dignity. It wasn't going to happen. She couldn't stop staring at him. If she let him take her in his arms, she'd be lost. She teetered as she leaned against the hotel room wall.

"I'm...I'm fine. I—"

"Hold still," he said. She heard his bare feet slap against the carpeting as he grabbed the second robe out of the coat closet and brought it back to her. "If you don't want to do this, that's your decision, but I don't understand what's wrong."

She struggled into the thick terry robe as she tried to think of a response. He was staring at her as she retrieved the fabric belt and swathed herself in yards of fabric. Judging by his continuing erection, he liked what he saw, even if it was covered up from her neck to below her knees. He licked his bottom lip. Her mouth went dry. Damn it.

Of *course* the most attractive guy she'd been anywhere near a bed with in the past year was completely off-limits.

"You don't recognize me," she said.

"No, I don't," he said. "Is there a problem?"

"You might say that." She finally succeeded in knotting the belt of the robe around her waist, dropped the sheet at her feet and stuck out one hand. "Hi. I'm Kendall Tracy. I'm the interim GM of the San Francisco Miners." His eyes widened in shock. "Nice to meet you."

About the Author

Julie Brannagh has been writing since she was old enough to hold a pencil. She lives in a small town near Seattle, where she once served as a city council member and owned a yarn shop. She shares her home with a wonderful husband, two uncivilized Maine Coons, and a rambunctious chocolate Lab.

When she's not writing, she's reading or armchair-quarterbacking her favorite NFL team from the comfort of the family room couch. Julie is a Golden Heart finalist and the author of contemporary sports romances.

Discover great authors, exclusive offers, and more at hc.com.

Give in to your impulses . . .
Read on for a sneak peek at six brand-new
e-book original tales of romance
from Avon Impulse.
Available now wherever e-books are sold.

AN HEIRESS FOR ALL SEASONS
A DEBUTANTE FILES CHRISTMAS NOVELLA
By Sophie Jordan

INTRUSION
AN UNDER THE SKIN NOVEL
By Charlotte Stein

CAN'T WAIT
A CHRISTMAS NOVELLA
By Jennifer Ryan

THE LAWS OF SEDUCTION
A FRENCH KISS NOVEL
By Gwen Jones

SINFUL REWARDS 1
A BILLIONAIRES AND BIKERS NOVELLA
By Cynthia Sax

SWEET COWBOY CHRISTMAS
A SWEET, TEXAS NOVELLA
By Candis Terry

An Excerpt from

AN HEIRESS FOR ALL SEASONS
A Debutante Files Christmas Novella
by Sophie Jordan

Feisty American heiress Violet Howard swears she'll never wed a crusty British aristocrat. Will, the Earl of Moreton, is determined to salvage his family's fortune without succumbing to a marriage of convenience. But when a snowstorm strands Violet and Will together, their sudden chemistry will challenge good intentions. They're seized by a desire that burns through the night, but will their passion survive the storm? Will they realize they've found a love to last them through all seasons?

His eyes flashed, appearing darker in that moment, the blue as deep and stormy as the waters she had crossed to arrive in this country. "Who are you?"

"I'm a guest here." She motioned in the direction of the house. "My name is V—"

"Are you indeed?" His expression altered then, sliding over her with something bordering belligerence. "No one mentioned that you were an American."

Before she could process that statement—or why he should be told of anything—she felt a hot puff of breath on her neck.

The insolent man released a shout and lunged. Hard hands grabbed her shoulders. She resisted, struggling and twisting until they both lost their balance.

Then they were falling. She registered this with a sick sense of dread. He grunted, turning slightly so that he took the brunt of the fall. They landed with her body sprawled over his.

Her nose was practically buried in his chest. *A pleasant smelling chest.* She inhaled leather and horseflesh and the warm saltiness of male skin.

He released a small moan of pain. She lifted her face to observe his grimace and felt a stab of worry. Absolutely mis-

SOPHIE JORDAN

placed considering this situation was his fault, but there it was nonetheless. "Are you hurt?"

"Crippled. But alive."

Scowling, she tried to clamber off him, but his hands shot up and seized her arms, holding fast.

"Unhand me! Serves you right if you are hurt. Why did you accost me?"

"Devil was about to take a chunk from that lovely neck of yours."

Lovely? He thinks she is lovely? Or rather her neck is lovely? This bold specimen of a man in front of her, who looks as though he has stepped from the pages of a Radcliffe novel, thinks that plain, in-between Violet is lovely.

She shook off the distracting thought. Virile stable hands like him did not look twice at females like her. No. Scholarly bookish types with kind eyes and soft smiles looked at her. Men such as Mr. Weston who saw beyond a woman's face and other physical attributes.

"I am certain you overreacted."

He snorted.

She arched, jerking away from him, but still he did not budge. His hands tightened around her. She glared down at him, feeling utterly discombobulated. There was so *much* of him—all hard male and it was pressed against her in a way that was entirely inappropriate and did strange, fluttery things to her stomach. "Are you planning to let me up any time soon?"

His gaze crawled over her face. "Perhaps I'll stay like this forever. I rather like the feel of you on top of me."

She gasped.

He grinned then and that smile stole her breath and made all her intimate parts heat and loosen to the consistency of pudding. His teeth were blinding white and straight set against features that were young and strong and much too handsome. And there were his eyes. So bright a blue their brilliance was no less powerful in the dimness of the stables.

Was this how girls lost their virtue? She'd heard the stories and always thought them weak and addle-headed creatures. How did a sensible female of good family cast aside all sense and thought to propriety?

His voice rumbled out from his chest, vibrating against her own body, shooting sensation along every nerve, driving home the realization that she wore nothing beyond her cloak and night rail. No corset. No chemise. Her breasts rose on a deep inhale. They felt tight and aching. Her skin felt like it was suddenly stretched too thin over her bones. "You are not precisely what I expected."

His words sank in, penetrating through the fog swirling around her mind. Why would he expect anything from her? He did not know her.

His gaze traveled her face and she felt it like a touch—a caress. "I shall have to pay closer attention to my mother when she says she's found someone for me to wed."

Violet's gaze shot up from the mesmerizing movement of his lips to his eyes. "Your *mother*?"

He nodded. "Indeed. Lady Merlton."

"Are you . . ." she choked on halting words. *He couldn't be.* "You're the—"

"The Earl of Merlton," he finished, that smile back again, wrapping around the words as though he was supremely amused. As though she were the butt of some grand jest. He was the Earl of Merlton, and she was the heiress brought here to tempt him.

A jest indeed. It was laughable. Especially considering the way he looked. Temptation incarnate. She was not the sort of female to tempt a man like him. At least not without a dowry, and that's what her mother was relying upon.

"And you're the heiress I've been avoiding," he finished.

If the earth opened up to swallow her in that moment, she would have gladly surrendered to its depths.

An Excerpt from

INTRUSION
An Under the Skin Novel
by Charlotte Stein

I believed I would never be able to trust any
man again. I thought so with every fiber of my
being—and then I met Noah Gideon Grant.
Everyone says he's dangerous. But the thing is
. . . I think something happened to him too. I
know the chemistry between us isn't just in my
head. I know he feels it, but he's holding back.
He's made a labyrinth of himself. Now all I
need to do is dare to find my way through.

An Avon Red Novel

He said no sexual contact, and a handshake apparently counts. I should respect that—I do respect that, I swear. I can respect it, no matter how much my heart sinks or my eyes sting at a rejection that isn't a rejection at all.

I can do without. I'm sure I can do without, all the way up to the point where he says words that make my heart soar up, up toward the sun that shines right out of him.

"Kissing is perfectly okay with me," he murmurs, and then, oh, God, then he takes my face in his two good hands, roughened by all the patient and careful fixing he does and so tender I could cry, and starts to lean down to me. Slowly at first, and in these hesitant bursts that nearly make my heart explode, before finally, Lord; finally, yes, finally.

He closes that gap between us.

His lips press to mine, so soft I can barely feel them. Yet somehow, I feel them everywhere. That closemouthed bit of pressure tingles outward from that one place, all the way down to the tips of my fingers and the ends of my toes. I think my hair stands on end, and when he pulls away it doesn't go back down again.

No part of me will ever go back down again. I feel dazed in the aftermath, cast adrift on a sensation that shouldn't have happened. For a long moment I can only stand there in stunned silence, sort of afraid to open my eyes in case the spell is broken.

But I needn't have worried—he doesn't break it. His expression is just like mine when I finally dare to look, full of shivering wonder at the idea that something so small could be so powerful. We barely touched and yet everything is suddenly different. My body is alight. I think his body is alight.

How else to explain the hand he suddenly pushes into my hair? Or the way he pulls me to him? He does it like someone lost at sea, finally seeing something he can grab on to. His hand nearly makes a fist in my insane curls, and when he kisses me this time there is absolutely nothing chaste about it. Nothing cautious.

His mouth slants over mine, hot and wet and so incredibly urgent. The pressure this time is almost bruising, and after a second I could swear I feel his tongue. Just a flicker of it, sliding over mine. Barely anything really, but enough to stun me with sensation. I thought my reaction in the movie theater was intense.

Apparently there's another level altogether—one that makes me want to clutch at him. I need to clutch at him. My bones and muscles seem to have abandoned me, and if I don't hold on to something I'm going to end up on the floor. Grabbing him is practically necessary, even though I have no idea where to grab.

He put his hand in my hair. Does that make it all right to put mine in his? I suspect not, but have no clue where that leaves me. Is an elbow any better? What about his upper arm? His upper arm is hardly suggestive at all, yet I can't quite bring myself to do it. If I do he might break this kiss, and I'm just not ready for that.

I probably won't be ready for that tomorrow. His stubble is burning me just a little and the excitement is making me so shaky I could pass for a cement mixer, but I still want it to carry on. Every new thing he does is just such a revelation—like when he turns a little and just sort of catches my lower lip between his, or caresses my jaw with the side of his thumb.

I didn't think he had it in him.

It could be that he doesn't. When he finally comes up for air he has to kind of rest his forehead against mine for a second. His breathing comes in erratic bursts, as though he just ran up a hill that isn't really there. Those hands in my hair are trembling, unable to let go, and his first words to me blunder out in guttural rush.

"I wasn't expecting that to be so intense," he says, and I get it then. He didn't mean for things to go that way. They just got out of control. All of that passion and urgency isn't who he is, and now he wants to go back to being the real him. He even steps back, and straightens, and breathes long and slow until that man returns.

Now he is the person he wants to be: stoic and cool. Or at least, that's what I think until he turns to leave. He tells me good-bye and I accept it; he touches my shoulder and I process this as all I might reasonably expect in the future. And then just as he's almost gone I happen to glance down, and see something that suggests that the idea of a real him may not be so clear-cut:

The outline of his erection, hard and heavy against the material of his jeans.

An Excerpt from

CAN'T WAIT
A Christmas Novella
by Jennifer Ryan

(Previously appeared in the anthology
All I Want for Christmas Is a Cowboy)

*Before The Hunted Series, Caleb and Summer
had a whirlwind romance not to be forgotten . . .*

Caleb Bowden has a lot to thank his best friend,
Jack, for—saving his life in Iraq and giving him
a job helping to run his family's ranch. Jack also
introduced Caleb to the most incredible woman
he's ever met. Too bad he can't ask her out. You
do not date your best friend's sister. Summer
and Caleb share a closeness she's never felt
with anyone, but the stubborn man refuses to
turn the flirtatious friendship into something
meaningful. Frustrated and tired of merely
wishing to be happy, Caleb tells Jack how he feels
about Summer. With his friend's help, he plans a
surprise Christmas proposal she'll never forget—
because he can't wait to make her his wife.

Caleb opened his mouth to yell, *Where the hell do you think you're going?*

He snapped his jaw shut, thinking better of it. He couldn't afford to let Jack see how much Summer meant to him. He'd thought he'd kept his need for her under wraps, but the too-observant woman had his number. Over the last few months, the easy friendship they'd shared from the moment he stepped foot on Stargazer Ranch turned into a fun flirtation he secretly wished could turn into something more. The week leading up to Thanksgiving brought that flirtation dangerously close to crossing the line when he walked through the barn door and didn't see her coming out due to the changing light. They crashed into each other. Her sweetly soft body slammed full-length into his and everything in him went hot and hard. Their faces remained close when he grabbed her shoulders to steady her. For a moment, they stood plastered to each other, eyes locked. Her breath stopped along with his and he nearly kissed her strawberry-colored lips to see if she tasted as sweet as she smelled.

Instead of giving in to his baser need, he leashed the beast and gently set her away, walking away without even a single word. She'd called after him, but he never turned back.

Thanksgiving nearly undid him. She'd sat alone in the dining room and all he'd wanted to do was be with her. But how could he? You do not date your best friend's sister. Worse, you do not have dangerous thoughts of sleeping with her, let alone dreaming of a life with a woman kinder than anyone he'd ever met. Just being around her made him feel lighter. She brightened the dark world he'd lived in for too long.

He needed to stay firmly planted on this side of the line. Adhere to the best-bro code. This thing went beyond friendship. Jack was his boss and had saved his life. He owed Jack more than he could ever repay.

"Can you believe her?" Jack pulled him out of his thoughts. He dragged his gaze from Summer's retreating sweet backside.

"Who's the guy?" He kept his tone casual.

Jack glared. "Ex-boyfriend from high school," he said, irritated. "He's home from grad school for the holiday."

"Probably looking for a good time."

Caleb tried not to smile when Jack growled, fisted his hands, and stepped off the curb, following after his sister. He'd counted on Jack's protective streak to allow him to chase Summer himself. Caleb didn't want anyone to hurt her. He sure as hell didn't want her rekindling an old flame with some ex-lover.

He and Jack walked into the park square just as everyone counted down, three, two, one, and the multicolored lights blinked on, lighting the fourteen-foot tree in the center of the huge gazebo, and sparking the carolers to sing "O Christmas Tree."

Tiny white lights circled up the posts and nearby trees, casting a glow over everything. The soft light made Summer's golden hair shine. She smiled with her head tipped back, her bright blue eyes glowing as she stared at the tree.

His temper flared when the guy hooked his arm around her neck and pulled her close, nearly spilling his beer down the front of her. She laughed and playfully shoved him away. The guy smiled and put his hand to her back, guiding her toward everyone's favorite bar. Several other people joined their small group.

Caleb tapped Jack's shoulder and pointed to Summer's back. Her long hair was bundled into a loose braid he wanted to unravel and then run his fingers through the silky strands.

"There she goes."

"What the . . . Let's go get her."

Caleb grabbed Jack's shoulder. "If you go in there and demand she leaves, it'll only embarrass her in front of all her friends. Let's scout the situation. Lie low."

"You're right. She'll only fight harder if we demand she come home. Let's get a beer."

Caleb grimaced. Hell yes, he wanted to drag Summer home, but fought the compulsion.

He did not want to watch her with some other guy.

Why did he torture himself like this?

An Excerpt from

THE LAWS OF SEDUCTION
A French Kiss Novel
by Gwen Jones

In the final fun and sexy French Kiss novel,
sparks fly as sassy lawyer Charlotte Andreko
and Rex Renaud, the COO of Mercier
Shipping, race to clear his name after he's
arrested for a crime he didn't commit.

An Excerpt from

THE LAWS OF SEDUCTION

A French Kiss Novel

by Gwen Jones

In her fifteen years as an attorney, Charlotte had never let anyone throw her off her game, and she wasn't about to let it happen now.

So why was she shaking in her Louboutins?

"Put your briefcase and purse on the belt, keys in the tray, and step through," the officer said, waving her into the metal detector.

She complied, cold washing through her as the gate behind her clanged shut. She glanced over her shoulder, thinking how much better she liked it when her interpretation of "bar" remained figurative.

"Name . . . ?" asked the other cop at the desk.

"Charlotte Andreko."

He ran down the list, checking her off, then held out his hand, waggling it. "Photo ID and attorney card."

She grabbed her purse from the other side of the metal detector and dug into it, producing both. After the officer examined them, he sat back with a smirk. "So you're here for that Frenchie dude, huh? What's he—some kinda big deal?"

She eyed him coolly, hefting her briefcase from the belt. "They're all just clients to me."

"That so?" He dropped his gaze, fingering her IDs. "How come he don't have to sit in a cell? Why'd he get a private room?"

Why are you scoping my legs, you big douche? "It's your jail. Why'd you give him one?"

He cocked a brow. "You're pretty sassy, ain't you?"

"And you're wasting my time," she said, swiping back her IDs. *God, it's times like these I really hate men.* "Are you going to let me through or what?"

He didn't answer. He just leered at her with that simpering grin as he handed her a visitor's badge, reaching back to open the next gate.

"Thank you." She clipped it on, following the other cop to one more door at the other side of the vestibule.

"It's late," the officer said, pressing a code into a keypad, "so we can't give you much time."

"I won't need much." After all, how long could it take to say *no fucking way*?

"Then just ring the buzzer by the door when you're ready to leave." When he opened the door and she stepped in, her breath immediately caught at the sight of the man behind it. She clutched her briefcase so tightly she could feel the blood rushing from her fingers.

"*Bonsoir*, Mademoiselle Andreko," Rex Renaud said.

Even with his large body cramped behind a metal table, the Mercier Shipping COO had never looked more imposing—

and, in spite of his circumstances, never more elegant. The last time they'd met had been in Boston, negotiating the separation terms of his company's lone female captain, Dani Lloyd, who had recently become Marcel Mercier's wife. With his cashmere Kiton bespoke now replaced by Gucci black tie, he struck an odd contrast in that concrete room, yet still exuded a coiled and barely contained strength. He folded his arms across his chest as his black eyes fixed on hers, Charlotte getting the distinct impression he more or less regarded her as cornered prey.

All at once the door behind her slammed shut, and her heart beat so violently she nearly called the officer back. Instead she planted her heels and forced herself to focus, staring the Frenchman down. "All right, I'm here," she said *en français*. "Not that I know why."

If there was anything she remembered about Rex Renaud—and he wasn't easy to forget—it was how lethally he wielded his physicality. How he worked those inky eyes, jet-black hair and Greek-statue handsomeness into a kind of immobilizing presence, leaving her weak in the knees every time his gaze locked on hers. Which meant she needed to work twice as hard to keep her wits sharp enough to match his, as no way would she allow him the upper hand.

An Excerpt from

SINFUL REWARDS 1
A Billionaires and Bikers Novella
by *Cynthia Sax*

Belinda "Bee" Carter is a good girl; at least, that's
what she tells herself. And a good girl deserves
a nice guy—just like the gorgeous and moody
billionaire Nicolas Rainer. Or so she thinks,
until she takes a look through her telescope
and sees a naked, tattooed man on the balcony
across the courtyard. He has been watching
her, and that makes him all the more enticing.
But when a mysterious and anonymous text
message dares her to do something bad, she
must decide if she is really the good girl she has
always claimed to be, or if she's willing to risk
everything for her secret fantasy of being watched.

An Avon Red Novella

I'd told Cyndi I'd never use it, that it was an instrument purchased by perverts to spy on their neighbors. She'd laughed and called me a prude, not knowing that I was one of those perverts, that I secretly yearned to watch and be watched, to care and be cared for.

If I'm cautious, and I'm always cautious, she'll never realize I used her telescope this morning. I swing the tube toward the bench and adjust the knob, bringing the mysterious object into focus.

It's a phone. Nicolas's phone. I bounce on the balls of my feet. This is a sign, another declaration from fate that we belong together. I'll return Nicolas's much-needed device to him. As a thank you, he'll invite me to dinner. We'll talk. He'll realize how perfect I am for him, fall in love with me, marry me.

Cyndi will find a fiancé also—everyone loves her—and we'll have a double wedding, as sisters of the heart often do. It'll be the first wedding my family has had in generations.

Everyone will watch us as we walk down the aisle. I'll wear a strapless white Vera Wang mermaid gown with organza and lace details, crystal and pearl embroidery accents, the bodice fitted, and the skirt hemmed for my shorter height. My hair will be swept up. My shoes—

Voices murmur outside the condo's door, the sound piercing my delightful daydream. I swing the telescope upward, not wanting to be caught using it. The snippets of conversation drift away.

I don't relax. If the telescope isn't positioned in the same way as it was last night, Cyndi will realize I've been using it. She'll tease me about being a fellow pervert, sharing the story, embellished for dramatic effect, with her stern, serious dad—or, worse, with Angel, that snobby friend of hers.

I'll die. It'll be worse than being the butt of jokes in high school because that ridicule was about my clothes and this will center on the part of my soul I've always kept hidden. It'll also be the truth, and I won't be able to deny it. I am a pervert.

I have to return the telescope to its original position. This is the only acceptable solution. I tap the metal tube.

Last night, my man-crazy roommate was giggling over the new guy in three-eleven north. The previous occupant was a gray-haired, bowtie-wearing tax auditor, his luxurious accommodations supplied by Nicolas. The most exciting thing he ever did was drink his tea on the balcony.

According to Cyndi, the new occupant is a delicious piece of man candy—tattooed, buff, and head-to-toe lickable. He was completing armcurls outside, and she enthusiastically counted his reps, oohing and aahing over his bulging biceps, calling to me to take a look.

I resisted that temptation, focusing on making macaroni and cheese for the two of us, the recipe snagged from the diner my mom works in. After we scarfed down dinner, Cyndi licking her plate clean, she left for the club and hasn't returned.

Three-eleven north is the mirror condo to ours. I

straighten the telescope. That position looks about right, but then, the imitation UGGs I bought in my second year of college looked about right also. The first time I wore the boots in the rain, the sheepskin fell apart, leaving me barefoot in Economics 201.

Unwilling to risk Cyndi's friendship on "about right," I gaze through the eyepiece. The view consists of rippling golden planes, almost like . . .

Tanned skin pulled over defined abs.

I blink. It can't be. I take another look. A perfect pearl of perspiration clings to a puckered scar. The drop elongates more and more, stretching, snapping. It trickles downward, navigating the swells and valleys of a man's honed torso.

No. I straighten. This is wrong. I shouldn't watch our sexy neighbor as he stands on his balcony. If anyone catches me . . .

Parts 1, 2, 3, 4, and 5 available now!

An Excerpt from

SWEET COWBOY CHRISTMAS
A Sweet, Texas Novella
by *Candis Terry*

Years ago, Chase Morgan gave up his Texas life
for the fame and fortune of New York City, and
he never planned on coming back—especially
not for Christmas. But when his life is turned
upside down, he finds himself at the door of sexy
Faith Walker's Magic Box Guest Ranch. Chase is
home for Christmas, and it's never been sweeter.

Chase had come up to stand beside her and hand her more ornaments. While most of the influential men who visited the ranch usually reeked of overpowering aftershave, Chase wore the scent of warm man and clean cotton. Tonight, when he'd shown up in a pair of black slacks and a black T-shirt, she'd had to find a composure that had nothing to do with his rescuing her.

She'd taken a fall all right.

For him.

Broken her own damn rules is what she'd done. Hadn't she learned her lesson? Men with pockets full of change they threw around like penny candy at a parade weren't the kind she could ever be interested in.

At least never again.

Trouble was, Chase Morgan was an extremely sexy man with bedroom eyes and a smile that said he could deliver on anything he'd promise in that direction. Broad shoulders that confirmed he could carry the weight of the world if need be. And big, capable hands that had already proven they could catch her if she fell.

He was trouble.

And she had no doubt she was in trouble.

Best to keep to the subject of the charity work and leave the drooling for some yummy, untouchable movie star like Chris Hemsworth or Mark Wahlberg.

Discreetly, she moved to the other side of the tree and hung a pinecone Santa on a higher branch. "We also hold a winter fund-raiser, which is what I'm preparing for now."

"What kind of fund-raiser?" he asked from right beside her again, with that delicious male scent tickling her nostrils.

"We hold it the week before Christmas. It's a barn dance, bake sale, auction, and craft fair all rolled into one." She escaped to the other side of the tree, but he showed up again, hands full of dangling ornaments. "Last year we raised $25,000. I'd like to top that this year if possible."

"You must have a large committee to handle all that planning."

She laughed.

Dark brows came together over those green eyes that had flashes of gold and copper near their centers. "So I gather you're not just the receptionist-slash–tree decorator."

"I have a few other talents I put to good use around here."

"Now you've really caught my interest."

To get away from the intensity in his gaze, she climbed up the stepstool and placed a beaded-heart ornament on the tree. She could only imagine how he probably used that intensity to cut through the boardroom bullshit.

As a rule, she never liked the clientele to know she was the sole owner of the ranch. Even though society should be living in this more open-minded century, there were those who believed it was still a man's world.

"Oh, it's really nothing that special," she said. "Just some odds and ends here and there."

When she came down the stepstool, his hands went to her waist to provide stability. At least that's what she told herself, even after those big warm palms lingered when she'd turned around to face him.

"Fibber," he said while they were practically nose to nose.

"I beg your pardon?"

"You know what I do for a living, Faith? How I've been so successful? I read people. I come up with an idea, then I read people for how they're going to respond. Going into a pitch, I know whether they're likely to jump on board or whether I need to go straight to plan B."

His grip around her waist tightened, and the fervor with which he studied her face sent a shiver racing down her spine. There was nothing threatening in his eyes or the way his thumbs gently caressed the area just above the waistband of her Wranglers.

Quite the opposite.

"You have the most expressive face I've ever seen," he declared. "And when you're stretching the truth, you can't look someone in the eye. Dead giveaway."

"And you've known me for what? All of five minutes?" she protested.

One corner of his masculine lips slowly curved into a smile. "Guess that's just me being presumptuous again."

Everything female in Faith's body awakened from the death sleep she'd put it in after she'd discovered the man she'd been just weeks away from marrying, hadn't been the man she'd thought him to be at all.

"Looks like we're both a little too trigger-happy in the jumping-the-gun department," she said, while deftly extricating herself from his grasp even as her body begged her to stay put.

"Maybe."

Backing away, she figured she'd tempted herself enough for one night. Best they get dinner over with before she made some grievous error in judgment she'd never allow herself to forget.

She clapped her hands together. "So . . . how about we get to that dinner?"

"Sounds great." His gaze wandered all over her face and body. "I'm getting hungrier by the second."

Whoo boy.